Elise Cooper

The Queen's Innocent

With other Poems

Elise Cooper

The Queen's Innocent
With other Poems

ISBN/EAN: 9783337206543

Printed in Europe, USA, Canada, Australia, Japan

Cover: Foto ©Andreas Hilbeck / pixelio.de

More available books at **www.hansebooks.com**

THE QUEEN'S INNOCENT

WITH OTHER POEMS

BY

ELISE COOPER

LONDON

DAVID STOTT, 370, OXFORD STREET, W

1886

CONTENTS

THE QUEEN'S INNOCENT.

Dramatis Personæ.

GLADYS, The Queen.

AON, The Prince, husband of the Queen.

CLEODORA, The Princess, sister of the Prince.

SIBYL
VERONICA } Ladies in attendance on the Princess.

PHARAMOND, Count of Ghyl, Cousin of the Queen and
Pretender to the Throne.

WITHOLD, Cousin of the Pretender.

TIMOTHY, a Tinker.

MORRA, a deformed girl, daughter of Timothy.

A Minister of State; A Gentleman of the household;
Courtiers; Officers; A Priest; Village folk.

BEN EPHRAIM, The Queen's Physician.

NARDI, THE QUEEN'S INNOCENT.

Scene:

*Partly in and about a Country Palace among the hills,
and partly in the Fortress of Sars.*

THE QUEEN'S INNOCENT.

—※—

ACT I.

Scene I.—A Room in the Palace.

Enter on one side the QUEEN *and the* PRINCE, *dressed for riding ; on the other a* MINISTER OF STATE.

MIN.   Good morning to my Sovereign and her spouse.
"How does your Majesty?" I need not ask.
  Your cheeks are ruddy with the rose of health,
  And happy lights are dancing in your eyes.
QUEEN.   And where, my Lord, should ruddier roses
    bloom,
  And where be seen to sparkle happier lights,
  Than in the face of one who grew a wife
  But three days since?
PRINCE.   His lordship's eye is grave.
  I hope he brings us no chill news to nip
  Your roses.

B

MIN.   Gravest looks may well reflect
　　The import of such tidings as I bear.
　　That insurrection, which we thought was quelled
　　Nine months ago, has broken forth afresh.
　　Madam, the base Pretender, with a force
　　Small but compact, has flung himself once more
　　Across the frontier, this time in the east ;
　　And, gathering augmentations by the way,—
　　For all the villages along his route
　　Declared for him at once—has marched to Sars,
　　Where, treachery having entered in advance,
　　After the merest semblance of a siege
　　The garrison has surrendered to him.
QUEEN.   Sars !
　　Why, one day's march, and he is quartered here,
　　Here in the Palace !
MIN.   He has done his worst
　　And utmost for the present.   Not the less
　　It is to be desired the court should move
　　Back to the capital without delay.
　　The public mind will be disquieted
　　Unless the Royal safety is secure.
QUEEN.   *We* fly before the face of Pharamond ? --
　　Not were he standing at our Palace gate !
　　This is to be a genuine honeymoon.

It's honey will not taste less sweet to me
For being gathered upon danger's brink.
Will it to you ? (*turning to the* PRINCE).
PRINCE.   My queen-bee, no.   Yet pause,
Were it not well to be advised?   Reflect———
QUEEN.   You fear these rebels then ?
PRINCE.   *I* fear them ?   No.
QUEEN.   Then let our cousin menace as he may,
Here we abide.   I like the neighbourhood
Of peril—not that this is truly such—
I will have up more troops, and make a wall
Of solid soldiery 'twixt Sars and us,
Behind whose cover we will walk and drive,
Hunt in the forest, paddle on the lake,
Enjoy our country pastimes just the same
As if Prince Pharamond were an honest man
And loyal subject.
MIN.   Madam, you are young.
PRINCE.   But were there none their progress to oppose?
How was this fortress garrisoned ?   You spoke
Of treachery——
QUEEN.   Yes, keep nothing back, my lord.
I thought that General Morios was at Sars?
MIN.   He is there still.
QUEEN.   A prisoner ?

MIN.   No.

QUEEN.   How then,

    Traitor ?   .   .   .

    (*To the* PRINCE.) We owe a woman thanks for this.

    Morios, grey-haired long since and past his prime,

    Has taken to himself of late a wife,

    Lovely, but of ignoble origin

    And infamous repute.   She, not content

    With leading thus in lawful life-long chains

    The greatest soldier of the state and time,

    Aspired to flaunt her beauty at the Court ;

    And he, presuming on his services,

    Required (infatuate !) she should be received,

    And chafed beneath my " No "—his first defeat.

MIN.   His single loss outweighs for us the entire

    Defection of an army.

QUEEN.   It was pricked—

    His loyalty ; it would not else collapse

    Thus at the first slight pressure.   Let him go.

    My lord, I think our council meets at three ;

    Till then, adieu.   (*Exit* MINISTER.)

PRINCE.   How long is it ago

    Since Pharamond sought your love ?

QUEEN.   My hand, you mean.

    You know that when the duke, my father, died,

Before his brother the unmarried king,
(The death of Dorion, my father's sole
Male issue, having anteceded his)—
PRINCE.   Dorion, your little step-brother.
QUEEN.   The same,—
  The supreme council of the realm repealed
  The law excluding females from the throne ;
  Wherefore the crown's reversion fell to me,
  Instead of Pharamond, the next heir male.
  For many a sharp offence against the laws,
  This Pharamond was then a banished man.
  His term of exile ended, he returned,
  (That was at my accession), saw me crowned,
  And swore allegiance.   When he deemed the way
  Sufficiently prepared for such a step,
  He asked my hand in marriage.   Then it was,
  Then, when despite the artful eloquence
  With which 'twas urged he saw his suit declined,
  Not without scorn, at once he dropped his mask,
  That southern province where his mother's house
  Had long upheld the old religion sought,
  And there, among the partisans of both,
  An army raised and had himself proclaimed
  King by the ancient law and right divine.
PRINCE.   A gambler, perjurer, and libertine ;

False, subtle, shifty and unscrupulous;—
What makes him popular with the multitude?

QUEEN. Liberal of hand when aught he has to give,
Liberal of promise when his purse is void,
Is Pharamond—the princely attribute
Of an imposing presence does not lack,
Nor yet a fluent and persuasive tongue,
And winning although studied courtesy
Of manner. With the multitude at large
That he is popular is not the truth.
His chief adherents are his mother's kin,
The clergy of the superseded faith,
Together with the unlettered peasant flock
They shepherd, and a malcontent or two
Like Morios.—Let us talk of him no more.
I long to be in the saddle, and I think
Our horses must by now be waiting. Goes
Cleodora with us?

PRINCE. No. I thought we two
Were company enough.

QUEEN. So failed to give
My message? Will you think thus three years hence?

[Exeunt.

SCENE II.—A LAWN SHADED BY TREES, WITH GARDEN-
CHAIRS AND A TABLE STREWN WITH BOOKS, NEEDLE-
WORK, A GUITAR, &c. PORTION OF THE PALACE, CON-
TAINING THE PRIVATE APARTMENTS OF THE *Princess*,
WITH A FLIGHT OF STEPS IN THE BACKGROUND. THE
Princess, Sibyl, AND *Veronica* DESCEND THE STEPS.

PRINCESS.   I wish to heaven the honeymoon were o'er,
And one could see, instead of those green glades,
The roofs and steeples of the capital.
I tire to death of this dull country life.
My brother is my brother now no more :
The Queen is grown his world, his universe ;
All others, be they whom they may, are nought—
The unknown beings in the farthest star
Can scarce concern him less.   While she is nigh
He has eluded death and is in heaven ;
Divorce him from her side a single hour—
He is an outcast angel, filled with gloom
And longing and disquietude, with eyes
Turned ever towards the gate of paradise,
Shut for the nonce.   I hate a man in love !
VERON.   They say that marriage is love's antidote.
The potion here has failed in its effect.
SIBYL.   Failed !   Why it has not yet had time to work.

How long have they been wedded ?   Just three days.
Oh, never fear but Hymen will restore
These victims whom the mischievous boy-god
Has bound and blinded.

VERON.   Yes ; no Eden long
Remains impenetrable to the snake.
I wonder through what dense hedge, lush with May,
Or verdurous wall of matted undergrowth,
Where even suspicion would not see the need
To halt or set a guard, his sinuous shape
Will bore an ingress to this paradise ?——
From underneath what bed of innocent flowers
His venom at this pair he first will dart ?
Oh, Sibyl, you and I will never wed !

PRINCESS.   I should have scoffed had anyone foretold
My brother thus infatuate could become !

SIBYL.   Your Highness thinks the Prince's love mis-
placed ?
The Queen not worth such ardent worship ?

PRINCESS.   Worth !
What lover looks at worth ?   There needs a net
Of brighter thread and subtler mesh than that,
To catch the vagrant fancy of a man.

VERON.   I wish I knew what sort of web to weave,
To snare so fine an insect——well-a-day !

A web spun out of thinnest star-beams, twined
With filaments of rose and sapphire mist?
SIBYL.   A less ethereal gossamer will trap
That butterfly.   To keep it afterwards
Alive, and never tear its fragile wings,
Or rub away the many-coloured dust
Which makes their beauty—that's the hardest thing.
I know not how our Prince got first enmeshed,
But scarcely wonder that he likes the net,
Once in it.
PRINCESS.   You admire the Queen, no doubt.
SIBYL.   I do.
VERON.   Her face is plain, you must allow.
SIBYL.   But was there ever so divine a smile?
VERON.   If its divinity would steal abroad
More often o'er her face, the smile might pass.
SIBYL.   Why now, I like that gentle gravity
Which overcasts her features when at rest.
The high responsibilities of power
Weigh on her youth a little heavily.
And then her voice —strong, silvery, musical ;
Susceptible of an infinitude
Of delicate modulations.
PRINCESS.   Voice is nought.
Men by the eye and not the ear are caught.

VERON.   Her figure is not good, you will admit.

SIBYL.   Not statuesque ; but then she bears herself
　　With such a grace and majesty as oft
　　The sculptor's model lacks.   She has the gift
　　Of manners—innate dignity with sweet
　　And gracious condescension blent.   In her
　　The queen and woman overlap, and melt
　　Into each other imperceptibly.

PRINCESS.   You look at objects through my brother's
　　　　glass.
　　You always did.   One focus suits you both.

VERON.   Sibyl has borrowed not the Prince's glass
　　Now, but his very eyes.

PRINCESS.　　　　　　　　I think she has.
　　What is she going to pay him for the loan ?
　　I recollect that once 'twas common talk——

SIBYL. (*quickly*).   Is it so strange that I admire the
　　　　Queen ?
　　Others, ere I, have recognized her charm,
　　Others have doted on her ere the Prince.
　　Pharamond, Count of Ghyl, as all the world
　　Well knows, once loved her,—

PRINCESS (*pale with anger*).   Sibyl, do you *dare*
　　Re-summon to my mind that episode ?
　　You know my vulnerable part, and there

You stab me.

SIBYL.   Your forgiveness I entreat.
But—prick me with the poniard, and I use
The poniard in defence.

PRINCESS.   'Twas policy,
Ambition—what you will, but never love.
His heart was faithful all the while to me.
I had not else forgiven him as I did.
Yet truly, as regards my brother's wife,
I like her not ; 'twixt her and me there lurks
Covert antagonism, some chymic law
Forbids our natures to amalgamate.
The smouldering fire nigh leapt into a blaze
But yesterevening, just because I shot
Some harmless pleasantries which had for aim
That simple youth they call "The Innocent."

VERON. Pity that so well-favoured a young man
Should lack the complement of all his wits.

PRINCESS. He might be less amusing were he more
Astute.   Much entertainment may be drawn
Out of his folly, I conceive.   The fool
Shall be our consolation while we stay
In this dull spot.   If but to spite the Queen,
With whom he seems a special favourite,
His witless head shall be our mark, whereat

Full many a lively shaft we three will wing.

SIBYL. Yes, only let the points be venomless.

Fool though he be, I thought he winced with pain

While you were making sport of him last night.

I had some talk about him yesterday

With that shrewd-faced old Jew with grizzled brows,—

PRINCESS. The Queen's physician?

SIBYL. Yes.

VERON. He has, they say,

Much influence in a certain quarter.

PRINCESS. Well?

Has he been always foolish, this young man?

SIBYL. He never has been quite as others are.

His fancy 's one of such a vivid sort,

He mixes with the phantasms of his sleep

The impressions of his waking hours, and this

The irrelevance his words and actions shew

In part, 'tis thought, accounts for. He was once

To fits of violence prone, but that 's long since,

His nature now is gentle,—though at worst

He wreaked no harm on any but himself—

And often you might talk to him for hours

And scarce his singularity perceive.

VERON. How came he to the court to be attached?

SIBYL. He sang beneath the windows of an inn

In which the Queen once rested for a night
While making a state-progress through the realm,
Soon after her accession to the throne.
Struck with his voice she sent for him, and straight
Conceived so great a fancy for the child
That, learning he was orphaned and as good
As friendless, she adopted him forthwith
Into her household, and—but see who comes—
VERON. Nardi himself, our target in the flesh !

Enter the QUEEN'S INNOCENT, *richly dressed, with his
right hand full of flowers. He bows low to all three
ladies, and then approaches the* PRINCESS.

NARDI. This is the woodland flower of which I spoke,
The fairest that is native to these parts,
To which it seems, as far as I can learn,
Peculiar.
PRINCESS. Yes, the blossoms, it is true,
Are pretty, but I do not greatly care
For wild flowers.
NARDI. And I like them best of all.
Look at these lovely bells—could culture make
Their form or hue more perfect ?

PRINCESS.   They exhale
  A noisome odour—ph !

NARDI.   You find the scent
  Ungrateful ?   Why, to me it seems most sweet !
  Our peasants say it is medicinal.

PRINCESS.   Medicinal, perhaps—but 'tis not sweet.
  It makes my head ache.   Sibyl, take the flowers
  And place them where their breath may not infect
  The air about me.   And, Veronica,
  Give me my smelling-bottle.
       (To NARDI, *after a pause.)*   I perceive
  Your eye has lighted on that instrument.
  They tell me you are musical.

NARDI.   Not so—
  Except in a poetic sort of way.
  Not truly musical.   I lack all skill
  That comes of intimate knowledge of the art ;
  To that I never could attain.

PRINCESS.   You play
  And sing, however?

NARDI.   To the Queen, sometimes—
  Who is too partial to be critical —
  And for my own poor pleasure when alone.

PRINCESS.   Will you vouchsafe · a sample of your
  powers?

(He takes the guitar and seats himself. Then, after a short prelude, sings :)

Is it not wintry chill on high
In that huge garden of the sky ?
  The roses said to the stars :
Why do you fold your petals bright—
Do you not love the glad daylight ?—
Until the sun has dropped from sight
  Behind the West's gold bars ?

Sweets do your lucent breasts immure
Which that small yellow epicure,
  The robber bee, discovers ?
Are beetles, burnished green, like those
That creep and in our hearts lie close,
Your nurslings ?—winds your playfellows ?—
  And nightingales your lovers ?

PRINCESS. Is that the end ? What poet made those
 words ?
NARDI. No poet, madam, saving I be one.
SIBYL. The song must surely have a sequel. What,
 In answer to the roses, said the stars ?

NARDI.   *(Changing the measure).*

Nor nurslings, nor playmates, nor lovers intrude
On our calm mid the vast of infinitude ;
    The stars to the roses said :
Nought have we that on us bee or beetle should doat
But we shine with our splendour undimmed when
    the note
Of your wooer, the nightingale, dies in his throat,
    And you roses are one and all dead.

The colour, the glow, pomp, and perfume of June,
Which you are a part of, is ended full soon,
    Summer, winter, autumnal and vernal
Each other succeed ; generations of roses
Bud, blossom and fade ; bloom decay presupposes :
While the summer with us neither varies nor closes,
    The season of prime is eternal.

VERON.   Sharp ears the stars and roses must have had,
    To hear each other such a space apart.
PRINCESS.   I do not care for poetry that deals
    Only with things inanimate.   Can you sing
    No human, passionate songs ?
NARDI.   Your Highness means . . . ?
SIBYL.   Her Highness means she likes Apollo best

In company with Eros.

NARDI.   What is he?

VERON.   Hear him!

SIBYL.   Oh, rightly named "The Innocent"!
You never heard of Eros?

NARDI.   If I did,
I have forgot.   Apollo, him I know.

SIBYL.   If one must clothe it in the vulgar tongue——
Her Highness means, can you not sing of love?

NARDI.   How can I sing of love
                Until its pangs I prove?
A temple not yet hallowed—such is my mute heart;
                A vacant pedestal,
                An empty shrine withal,—
How can I sing of love that know not love's sweet
                smart?

                The temple which to erect,
                Time, the still architect,
Has taken twice nine years, doth towards completion
                haste;
                But yet no goddess blest
                Makes herself manifest,
By vision or by voice, within the precincts chaste.

The shrine is carved—inwrought
With many a jewel-thought,
And many a flower-like rich emotion, fair devised,
But she for whom the hours
In silence thus their powers
Have plied, the holy saint, is still uncanonized.

The pedestal doth want
Its marble occupant ;
Perchance some opal dawn, not distant, may discover
The statue in its place
Upon the breathing base,
Sculptured with imagery of passionate dreams all over.

PRINCESS.   Shrine—temple—of his bosom's sanctity
  This youth a goodly notion entertains.
SIBYL.—A shrine 's a box, with gew-gaws overlaid,
  That holds dry bones.
VERON.   A temple is a place
  Where strange gods meet and jostle.   Sanctity !
SIBYL.   He calls his heart a sculptured pedestal ;
  That is to say his heart is made of stone.
VERON.   To boast himself thus hardened at eighteen !
NARDI.   Ladies, in future you shall sing yourselves.
  You mock at my poor efforts.

PRINCESS. Be not vexed.

They mock at all things, these wild girls of mine,

'Tis often but lip-mockery all the while.

I liked your last song better than the first.

NARDI. Teach me what kind of music you prefer,

And I will sing no other. Will you try

One little ditty? (*Offers her the guitar.*)

PRINCESS. Hand the instrument

To Lady Sibyl.

Sibyl, you who led

The laugh against him, give him his revenge.

SIBYL. Which shall I sing of all the songs I know?

VERON. "One little ditty!"

SIBYL. Merry shall it be,

Or sad? . . Alack, the youth looks critical!

SIBYL'S SONG.

Give me back the kisses which you stole;

The peace of mind you robbed me of restore;

Make me heart-whole,

Heart-free once more.

Weapons have been known that, with a touch,

The wounds aforetime they bestowed could heal;

My wound did such

A weapon deal.

C 2

Lay them back upon my lips again,
    All those kisses that by fraud were reft ;
And then—why then
        Repeat the theft !

PRINCESS.   A Sibylline conclusion.   Take this youth
    For pupil ; he already knows the knack
    Of stringing rhymes, now you can teach him style
    And sentiment.
SIBYL.   Oh, teaching's not my forte.
    Besides, his eyes are asking terms elsewhere.
    Ha ! ha ! I guess whose pupil he will be.
VERON (*who has taken up some needlework*).
    Where have my scissors wandered ?
          (*To the Princess*) Snip this thread,
    Here, with your dagger.
NARDI.   'Tis a dagger, then,
    Your Highness wears, and no mere ornament.
PRINCESS.   Both.   'Twas the fashion when I left my land
    To wear such baubles.   See, its edge is keen.
          (*Sheathes and hands it to him.*)
NARDI (*unsheathing and holding it up.*)
    Oh, how the bright steel flashes back the light !
    Just such another I should like to own.

PRINCESS. If you would like to keep it, it is yours.

NARDI. You mean it? But the hilt is jewelled. . . . No,
The gift is far too costly (*tenders it back*).

PRINCESS. View its gems
As guerdon for your singing and your flowers.

NARDI. Your Highness's acceptance of the one,
Approval of the other—such was all
The guerdon I desired.

SIBYL. A pretty speaker!

VERON. A very pretty!

PRINCESS. Well, receive it then
As a free gift, and wear it for my sake.

NARDI. I may not wear a weapon—that's the truth.
Her Majesty forbids—I know not why.

PRINCESS. Wear it behind her royal back.

NARDI. But—but—

PRINCESS. "But—but!" Oh, take or leave it, as you
choose (*rises*).

VERON. It's ill-luck giving sharp-edged tools. I wager
He cuts his fingers playing with that toy,
And then his blood will rest upon your head.

PRINCESS. Lightly, I think.

Re-enters the Palace, followed by SIBYL *and* VERONICA.
NARDI *stands gazing after them for a few seconds, then
lifts the dagger reverentially to his lips.*

Scene III.—A Corridor in the Palace.

Enter a Courtier *and an* Aide-de-Camp.

Court.   How long do you suppose that it will take
  To smoke these rebels out ?
Aide.   Two months, at least.
  Placed near the summit of a range of hills,
  Sars occupies a site well-nigh unmatched
  For natural strength.   It is impregnable,
  Moreover, on account of its deep ditch
  And scarps in masonry, to all assaults
  Save those conducted in a normal way—
  By means of an elaborate scheme, to wit,
  Of trenches, mines, and batteries, till, its walls
  Crumbling, our storming columns can advance
  Without more solid hindrance than the arms
  And bodies of the men defending it.
  The patient labour of the engineer,
  The moving up and planting on the heights
  Of heavy guns, asks time.   The stronghold once
  Retaken, the surrender of the town
  It overlooks and lords ensues, of course,
  With that of such entrenchments as remain.
Court.   I query whether Pharamond and his friends
  Will put your engineers to all this pains.

AIDE.   That hangs upon the course events may take
　　Elsewhere.   His unexpected spurt of luck
　　The Prince Pretender doubtless thinks will tempt
　　Some larger towns, in one or two of which
　　His secret agents an enthusiasm
　　Factitious are already churning up,
　　In favour of his title to pronounce.
　　This hope will prove illusory, I believe ;
　　Sars in the end must either yield or fall ;
　　A desultory warfare he may then
　　Maintain among the hills, till by degrees
　　His following melts away from him————
COURT.   Or else
　　Retreating, with his shavelings and his boors,
　　Into his own insurgent province, keep
　　That chronic sore from healing.
AIDE.   Be assured
　　The Government will never pause again
　　Till this revolt is finally stamped out.
COURT.   Who would have thought a tempest was to
　　　plough
　　The halcyonian waters, when we moored
　　The royal nuptial barge in this smooth spot
　　So few days since ?   Ah well, our country life
　　Is too much of one colour for my taste ;

This influx of the brave, the trampling past
Of regiments, martial glitter and parade,
The bustle and excitement and suspense
Whose centre we are like to be erelong,
Will streak it with fresh dyes.

AIDE.　　　　　　　　　　　I thought the Court
Was going back to town.

COURT.　　　　　　　　The Queen declares
She will at least stay out her honeymoon,
And would, were twenty Pharamonds in arms.

AIDE.　Brave lady.

COURT.　　　　　　Venus' doves can bill and coo
Though Mars be present.

AIDE.　　　　　　　Venus' doves were never
The birds to startle at the god of fight.　　[*Exeunt.*

SCENE IV.—A ROOM IN THE PALACE.

(QUEEN *at work upon a piece of tapestry;* NARDI, *on a low stool near her feet, sings to his guitar:*)

Were the lute of Orpheus mine,
I would haste where battle rages,
And, as host with host engages,
Play upon its strings divine

So sweetly, wildly—
  Mid the fierce unholy jar
Steal they should, those sounds, and drown
  The harsh music of dread war ;
Till the combatants laid down
    Their arms, and mildly
  Stood and gazed at one the other ;
And I would not cease from playing
Until each, instead of slaying,
  Clasped his foeman like a brother,
And wept sweet holy tears, and then
Turned home to till his fields again.

  Were the lute of Orpheus mine,
I the overhanging beak
Of some cape of storms would seek,
  On its giddiest verge recline,
    And there the dreaming
  Chords to notes so loud and clear
Waken, that for leagues around
  All the waves and winds should hear ;
And the sea-gulls at the sound
    Would hush their screaming,
  And the thunder faint would grow,

And the billow tame its crest,
And the surge from beating rest,
   And the tempest cease to blow ;
And ships in peril on the deep
Rock safe as babes that cradled sleep.

   Were the lute of Orpheus mine,
Playing always I would go
Through life's bye-ways to and fro,
   Working a result benign
      On whatsoever
   Chanced to hear the music sweet ;
Turmoil should give place to quiet ;
   Poverty's dry crust would eat
Equal to the daintiest diet ;
      Hard hearts that never
   Felt a thrill should melt with ruth ;
Misers, of their own accord,
With the needy share their hoard ;
   Liars fall in love with truth ;
The sick and sad forget their pain,
And wrinkled age grow young again.

NARDI.   Did Orpheus love Eurydice ?

QUEEN. He had.
A sort of kindness for her, I believe.

NARDI. I dreamt last night that I was Orpheus.

QUEEN. Yes?
Did many beasts collect to hear you sing?

NARDI. A panther came and crouched against my feet,
And as I sang it altered—guess to what?

QUEEN. A wolf?

NARDI. A woman.

QUEEN. A more perilous shape
It could not take. I hope you ran away.

NARDI (*crooning to himself.*)
Which were crueller of the two,
The panther or the woman?—
The beast's heart or the human?
I could tell methinks—could you?

QUEEN. Is that a question to be answered?

NARDI (*with a sudden vivacity*). Madam,
How like you being wedded?

QUEEN. Well enough.
The Prince and I have not been man and wife
So long we tire of one the other yet.

NARDI. I, too, would be beloved!

QUEEN. Why, so you are.
They get no grace from me that love you not.

NARDI.   But in the way you love the Prince I mean,
   As Orpheus by Eurydice was loved.
(BEN EPHRAIM, *the* QUEEN'S PHYSICIAN, *enters behind.*)
QUEEN.   What folly is fermenting in your brain?
   You think to love is to be blest?—you err.
   Two bitter drops to every one of sweet
   Compose that draught. Each rapture veils some pang.
   Fierce jealousies, wild angers, torturing doubts,
   All interweave their dark or lurid threads
   Amid the texture of the happiest love.
NARDI.   Can this be true?
QUEEN.   If ever you should meet
   Love in your wanderings, turn your back on him;
   Pause not to parley, do not give him time
   To throw his bandage round your eyes, but turn
   And resolutely flee.
NARDI.   But, madam, you
   Are happy? You would not with love dispense?
QUEEN.   Once captive to that lord we hug our chains.
   But you—keep free! Love's fetters seem of flowers,
   But 'neath his roses there are gyves of steel.
NARDI (*rising.*)   I take my leave.
QUEEN.   Where go you?
NARDI.   To the woods
   To meditate.   [*Exit* NARDI.

BEN E. An aged bachelor,
  It is so many decades since I paid
  Incense of futile sighs at Venus' shrine,
  I scarce remember what such worship means.
  But that was only sophistry, I hope,
  Which, falling from the lips of one on whom
  Wifehood so newly sits, I heard but now.
QUEEN. It was the truth. . . . Yet only half the truth.
BEN E. The other half?——
QUEEN. Corrects it—qualifies,
  And that shall Nardi never learn from me;
  Would there were none to teach it him beside.
  I have observed with some disquietude
  A change in him of late. His bearing shows
  A manlier and more gallant grace. His locks,
  That flowed untamed, are trimmed and curled with
    care.
  And he who gave so little thought to dress
  Now rivals, nay, eclipses, in his garb
  The foppishness of our court exquisites.
BEN E. Your Majesty, in dress, as other things,
  Permits him too much license. For the rest —
  All this is well; the boy becomes a man.
QUEEN. A man indeed, and yet it is not well.
  The advent of the Princess at our Court

Marks the commencement of this change.   He aims
At finding favour in her lovely eyes.

BEN E.   She and her ladies mock him openly !
I ventured in their hearing to remark
But yesterevening that in generous minds
The youth's simplicity was wont to breed
Consideration rather than contempt,
And that your Majesty would not endure
To see him made a sport of.   .

QUEEN.   Only note
His changeful cheek, the hunger in his eyes,
The while her smallest movement he observes,
Hangs breathless on her utterance.   Just pronounce
" Cleodora " or " the Princess," suddenly,
And see the hot blood flame up in his face !
By means of a profound and happy love
His wayward feet might find for good and all
The mother-level of humanity.
But this can never prove a happy love.
Think of the possibilities it implies,
The issues opens !   Why was he not smit
With some poor gentlewoman, whose estate
Might match with his?—some comely peasant even,
(Since he for persons owns not much respect),
Met in the woods ?   But no, his heart for mate

Demands a princess—thus imperiously
Will blood assert itself.   Ben Ephraim, mark—
He must be thwarted ere this goes too far.

BEN E.   It is some fantasy.   'Twill pass away
As other fantasies have passed before.

QUEEN.   For once your penetration is at fault.
This is no fantasy.

BEN E.   Whate'er it be,
It cannot flourish in the shrewd bleak air
Of scorn like hers.

QUEEN.   Be not too sure of that.
I have a black foreboding she is meant
To work some evil upon me and mine.
Why can I not be friends with her?   Why shuts
My heart at her approach—so beautiful
A being, sister of my own beloved?
Such beauty oft brings ruin, so they say.
You smile—old men forget they once were young.
Well, well—keep Nardi in your sight, that's all.

BEN E.   I strive to do so always.

QUEEN.   If he loves
He will grow subtle.   Do not let him hoodwink
Your vigilance (*rises to go*).   You ride this afternoon.
Far?

BEN E.   To within a brace of miles of Sars.

I go to see what change six months have wrought
Upon some forest patients.

QUEEN.   Look you keep
Clear of the rebel outposts, and beware
Of scouts and sharp-shooters.   Best take a guard.

BEN E.   I thank your Majesty.   My groom and I
Go both well armed.   [*Exeunt different ways.*

SCENE V.—BEFORE AN ALE-HOUSE ON THE VILLAGE
GREEN.   *Timothy* LIES DRUNK ON A BENCH WITH
HIS POTS AND PANS NEAR HIM.   ENTER VILLAGE
BOYS HUSTLING *Morra*, A DEFORMED GIRL, WHO
CARRIES A LOAD OF FIREWOOD.

BOYS.   Crook-back !   Crook-back !

MORRA.   You wicked boys !   You brutes !

TIMOTHY (*sitting up*).   Why, that's my Morra !   Hullo !
   . . How now, boys ?
Hold hard there !   .   .   .   (*Relapses.*)

   (*She struggles.   They strike and push her down.*)

A BOY.   Oh, oh !   She has bit my hand !
The young she-devil !   Duck her in the pond !

OTHER BOYS.   Yes, duck her in the pond, the ugly witch !

   (*They are dragging her away when* NARDI *enters.*
   BOYS *leave her and scamper off.*)

NARDI. Why were they going to duck you in the pond?

MORRA. Because I am crook'd and ugly—cause enough.

NARDI. Where do you live?

MORRA (*sullenly*).   What's that to you?

NARDI.   Not much.

   Only you seem so wretched and so poor,

   And I might help you if I knew the way.

   What are your friends?

MORRA (*still sullenly*). Got none. That's father, there—

   Drunk, as he most times is, along that bench.

   And grandf'er's childish, and a bed-licr.

NARDI. But tell me, do you get enough to eat?

   You look half-starved.

MORRA (*with a short laugh*). Why, often I could eat

   More than I get,—most poor folks can, no doubt.

   Grandf'er, he's always craving after food, —

   I go without, and let him have my share

   Besides his own, to quiet him sometimes.

   Father, he mostly lives upon the drink.

NARDI. What does he do then for a livelihood,

   That father?

MORRA. Tinkers pots and such like.

                  (*Shoulders her firewood.*)

NARDI.   Stay,

   That load 's too heavy for your poor back to bear.

Let me take part.   Well, I shall take the whole
Since you resist.   Now you go on in front,
And show the way.   I'll follow.

      (MORRA *sulkily obeys.   Exeunt.*)

TIMOTHY (*rousing himself again*).   Gently, boys,
Morra's a poor weak creature.   Not too rough.
   (*Becomes aware that he is alone.   Rises and with
    difficulty shoulders his pots.*)
Any pots to mend!   Any pots or pans to mend!

      (*Reels off.*)

SCENE VI.—AN ANTECHAMBER IN THE PALACE.   A
SOUND IS HEARD AS OF A KEY BEING TURNED IN A
LOCK.   A DOOR OPENS AND A GENTLEMAN OF THE
HOUSEHOLD ENTERS CAUTIOUSLY, FOLLOWED BY THE
Pretender.

GEN.   Her antechamber— this,
Behind yon door's her private sitting-room.
That other opens on the corridor.
Now hide behind this curtain.   Note—the key
Is in the lock.   In case of accident
Be sure to turn it, and arrest pursuit,
Ere you fly down the staircase.   Someone comes.
Heaven bless your Royal Highness and protect!

      ⌊*Exit* GENTLEMAN.

Enter SIBYL *and* VERONICA.

SIBYL.   But what a curious bend of circumstance
That sets the man, to whom for four long years
The Princess has been secretly betrothed,
In opposition to her brother's wife.
VERON.   He was in arms against the Queen before.
SIBYL.   The Queen was not then married to our Prince.
Then with the Count flew all our hopes abreast ;
Now some will lag upon uncertain wing—
The lover's gain must be the brother's loss.
VERON.   A brother counts for nought against a lover.
Besides, the Princess bears her sister-in-law,
And sometime rival, small good will, we know,
And would not greatly grieve to see the crown
Plucked from her brows.   'Tis true the Prince must
      yield
His share in that same bauble, but to whom ?
Aon to Cleodora would give way,
Prince Consort to Queen Consort ; hence say I,
" Success attend the arms of Pharamond ! "
PRET. (*aside.*) Amen, Veronica !
SIBYL.   He makes no sign,—
A victor and so near, and yet to send
No line of greeting, no mute token even !

The Princess feels it, though she nothing says.
When 'thwart what seemed his pathway to this throne
His heart is set on, Love stood heretofore,
Without remorse he bade it stand aside.
He once proved false—he may prove false again.

PRET. (*aside.*) The little traitress! I am like to meet
The common fate of listeners, I can see.

VERON. Oh, but their secret trothplight is not now
What then it was—a drag upon the wheel
Of his ambition. Present intercourse
Between them fraught with danger were to both.
Silence with him means prudence, nothing more.

SIBYL. What will not love adventure for the sake
Of one beloved ? I think if—

(*Perceives the* PRETENDER *emerging from behind the
curtain, and stops abruptly.* VERONICA *sees him
at the same moment and gives a faint shriek.*)

PRET.   Do not scream,
Or you betray me. Sibyl sweet, and dear
Veronica, my safety only lives
In your discretion.

VERON.   Is it you yourself,
And not your ghostly second ?

PRET.   Have no fear.
'Tis I, arrayed in honest flesh and blood.

SIBYL. How could your Highness run so great a risk ?

PRET.   Ah, Sibyl, you forget—"What will not love
Adventure for the sake of one beloved?"
Hark! is not that a step without I hear?

VERON.   (*who has run to the door to reconnoitre.*)
It's only Nardi.

SIBYL.   We will deal with him.
Conceal yourself behind the curtain—quick!
                The QUEEN'S INNOCENT *enters.*

NARDI.   Ladies, illustrious and dear, I deemed—

SIBYL.   Oh, Nardi, speak to us in prose, it's all
Flat prose with us to-day. What is 't you want?
You cannot see her Highness, she is sick.

NARDI.   Sick! She looked freshly as a new-blown rose
This noon. Not very sick, I trust?

SIBYL.   Why, no;
A headache,—yet most violent while it lasts.
Her brow feels fit to burst.

NARDI.   Is she in bed?

SIBYL.   No, but reclining.

NARDI.   Let me go to her!
The Queen, too, suffers thus, and always then
She has the chamber darkened, and I sit
And soothe her to repose with music soft.

VERON.   Oh really, what a gentle anodyne!
I warrant now she gets these headaches oft.

SIBYL.   Ah, but the Princess differs from the Queen.

She at such times unbroken silence needs.
Her chamber-woman scarce so much as dares
To cross—st!　Nardi!　Go not near that door,
Her ear is preternaturally acute.

NARDI.　And so is mine.　I heard a sound as if—

SIBYL.　It is he Highness groaning.

VERON.　　　　　　　　　　　　　　　Ay, to groan
She always says relieves her when she has
This toothache.

NARDI.　　　　　　Toothache?

VERON.　　　　　　　　　　　　　Well, and have we not
Been talking of the toothache all along?

SIBYL.　Poor lady, there—I hear her groan again.
This rheumatism is very hard to bear.
A sudden twinge will catch her in the side,—

NARDI (*looking from one to the other*).
My presence is inopportune, I see.
Why could you not have told me so at once?
You two gay ladies always mock at me.　　　[*Exit.*

(*The* PRETENDER, *who from his hiding-place has been regarding* NARDI *with a great deal of interest, comes forward.*)

PRET.　Who is that stripling?

VERON.　　　　　　　　　　　The Queen's Innocent.

PRET.　What?

Sibyl.   'Tis a name they give a simple youth
  Who dwells at Court protected by the Queen.
Veron.   In other words her fool, and (save the mark !)
  A rival of your Highness's.
Pret.   My rival?
Veron.   That little wicked wanton, Venus' son,
  Has set us playing at cross-purposes
  Within these walls.   Just now the game stands thus :
  The Princess loves your royal and gracious self;
  The Innocent the Princess.   Then the Prince,
  For all he 's married to her, loves the Queen ;
  The Queen the Innocent.   Our Sibyl, here,
  Adores in secret —
Sibyl.   Fie, Veronica !
  His Highness did not jeopardize his life
  To listen to such folly.   (*To the* Pretender.) Shall I warn
  The Princess you are here ?
Pret.   Ay Sibyl, do.
  I am on fire to see her.   Bid her haste.   [*Exit* Sibyl.
  And so the Queen is partial to this youth ?
Veron.   Yes ; if he were her spaniel or her ape,
  She could not pet him more.   I almost think
  Her Majesty would nurse him on her lap
  If he were not so big.

PRET.   A handsome lad.
　Is he of gentle birth?
VERON.   I cannot tell.
　Her Majesty got hold of him by chance.
　She heard him sing—or something—Sibyl knows.
　The Queen's physician—
PRET. (*starting*)   Ha! and what of him?
VERON.　Nothing.　'Twas he told Sibyl, that is all.
　　　(*Re-enter, from within,* SIBYL *with the* PRINCESS.)
PRINCESS (*with a cry*). Pharamond!
PRET.   My Cleodora! (*they embrace.*)
PRINCESS.   I began
　To think that we were never more to meet!
PR ET.　I fear you learn to nurse hard thoughts of me.
　The exigencies of the time compel—
PRINCESS.　Our love to walk by faith not sight, I know.
　'Tis hard—though this mends all.　But Pharamond,
　How could you penetrate within these walls?
　Would not your life be forfeit were you found?—
　I tremble.　How were you disguised to pass
　The sentries at the gates?　Oh, are you sure
　You were not recognized?
PRET.   Suffice it, sweet,
　Within these walls are some who wish me well.
　Through their connivance am I able thus

To enter on love's errand.

PRINCESS.   Wonderful!

'Tis like a dream, this meeting.

PRET.   Nay, to me

'Tis like the realization of a dream.

PRINCESS.   Oh, Pharamond, I have longed for you so

    oft.   . . . (*they embrace again.*)

Well, girls, what think you, has he altered much?

Come to the light.   I have not looked at you

For such a weary while! . . . How bronzed you are.

Heavens! is that grey amid your hair?

PRET.   No doubt.

SIBYL.   Frost in September!

VERON.   No, July—the height

Of summer!

PRET.   Oh, but you forget my years

Are eight-and-thirty.   Younger oft than I,

Do have to entertain these witnesses.

VERON.   False witnesses I call them, when they come

So early.

SIBYL.   I would rather pluck them out,

Were I his Highness, and go bald.

PRIN.   Oh dear!—

Do I look older?   Am I changed at all?

PRET. (*holding her at arms' length*) Changed as the year

  is changed, when April yields

To May—or as the opening lily-bud
When to the perfect blossom it expands.
My golden lily with the heart of fire!
My May incarnate, with for face a flower!
My full-grown, finished beauty! Small surprise
If lovers haunt your antechamber—one
Has just reluctantly gone hence.

Prin.   What, Nardi?
A very gentle and ingenuous youth.
'Tis true he loves me. Twenty times a day
The secret trembles to his lips, but shame
Hurries it, frightened, back into his heart.
In some unguarded moment out 'twill leap.
Ah! you do well to feel a jealous pang.
But come, I have a thousand things to ask——

Pret. Dear love, and I a thousand things to tell,
And all too brief a space to say them in.

Prin. Here from intrusion one is never safe.
Let us withdraw into my sitting-room.
Veronica and Sibyl, you remain,
And ward off all approach. Whoever comes,
Say I am sick, asleep, or what you will.

Sibyl. No pair of advocates could lie more glibly
Than we will for your Highness's behoof.

ACT II.

SCENE I.—A ROOM IN THE FORTRESS OF SARS.

(The PRETENDER *seated at one end of a table, the* QUEEN'S PHYSICIAN *standing at the other. A* SOLDIER *on guard at the door. The* PRETENDER *folds and seals a despatch he has been writing, and hands it to* WITHOLD, *who is in attendance, and who then withdraws, the* SOLDIER *following him.)*

PRET.   Doctor, the inconvenience we regret
To which, in consequence of having ridden
So near our outposts, you have been exposed.
We do not war with men of peace like you,
Even when they count themselves among our foes,
With either the physician or divine,—
Priest of men's bodies, doctor of men's souls,
We view them both as neutrals.   Sit, I pray.
                    (PHYSICIAN *declines by a gesture.*)
The hour is late.   Refreshment and repose
You need before your journey you retrace.
As soon as morning lights anew the skies
You shall be safely through our lines convoyed.

BEN E.   Your Highness is a courteous foe.

PRET.   But yet,
    The while your misadventure I deplore,
    I gladly seize the chance which it presents
    Of forming an acquaintance with a man
    Of such repute.   I dabbled, you must know,
    In medicine a little when a lad . . . .
    One of my whims . . . and I remember yet
    A treatise from your pen which then I read,
    And whence I drew much profit and delight.

BEN E.   Princes as well as parasites, I learn,
    Can flatter.

PRET.   In the art which you profess,
    By study and experience, you have gained
    Surprising skill and knowledge.   They do say
    That you can cause the dead to live once more.

BEN E.   My poor pretensions never stretched so far.

PRET.   My little kinsman for example, he
    That should have filled the throne if he had lived,
    Dorion, the brother of the Queen—'tis said
    A word from you could conjure him to life
    Before our startled eyes.

BEN E.   A pleasant jest.

PRET.   You err.   I speak in solemn seriousness.
    You are my royal cousin's trusted friend . . .

For still our cousinship I warmly feel,
Though she I think would wipe it if she could
Out of her visage, where 'tis stamped by God,
And though the exigencies of the hour,
My right and their's who after me may come,
Compel me to oppose her thus in arms.
Events might otherwise have shaped themselves,
Had she so willed. . . . I loved her—but that's
    past;
She would not view me even as a friend—
Yet who so fit to be her friend as I,
Allied in blood and feature?   Many have marked
The likeness—which is nothing wonderful,
Sprung as we are from brothers like as twins,
And she so favouring as she does her sire.

BEN E.   The features of her Majesty, indeed,
  Proclaim her without doubt her father's child.

PRET.   The little Prince inherited, I think,
  His mother's loveliness?

BEN E.   I scarce can say.
  Prince Dorion was a pretty boy enough,
  Though small and pale and sickly from his birth.

PRET.   There is a youth at Court, so gossip tells,
  Whose countenance bears a close similitude
  (Too close to be the mere result of chance),

To her's who was the step-dame of the Queen,
The lovely Princess round whose end there hung
Such mystery.

BEN E.   Truly?   Whom your Highness means
I cannot guess.

PRET.   Complexioned as the lily ;
With eyes of solemn tender grey, which flash
Innocuous lightnings like a summer night;
But all the gold of sunrise on his curls ;—
Know you none such, good Doctor ?

BEN E.   None indeed.
I did not think our gracious Sovereign's court
Hold such a beauty.

PRET.   Who and what is he
They nickname " The Queen's Innocent " ?

BEN E.   What, Nardi?

PRET.   Ay, Nardi.

BEN E.   'Tis at him your Highness points ?
And yet the lad is comely, it is true.
A poor half-witted youth, who when the Queen—

PRET.   Doctor Ben Ephraim, mark me—there are secrets
The which it might advantage me to know
And you to tell.   Full gladly would I sit
Of such a potent magus at the feet.
No premium you could ask I would not give,

Twice o'er, to purchase such apprenticeship.
This matter of my little cousin's death,—

BEN E.   Stay, Count of Ghyl, and once for all mark *me*.
I practise but I do not teach mine art.
My secrets, have I them, are not for sale.

PRET.   Of such an one as you are have I dreamed,
As standing by my side, my trusty friend,
My chiefest counsellor, with cunning hand
Helping me to mine own.

BEN E.   At seventy years,
It is too late allegiance to transfer.
I shall be satisfied to end my days
The servant of Queen Gladys.

PRET.   My claim rests
On justice and on immemorial law ;
None other are the Caryatids strong
Which do my cause sustain.

BEN E.   Your royal word
Is pledged that I am free to-morrow morn ?

PRET. (*after a slight pause as of indecision.*)
Our word is pledged and it shall be redeemed.

                    (*Blows a whistle.   Soldier re-appears.*)
Follow that soldier.   To your pillow, peace.
One moment.   Morning's thoughts do better oft
The night's—

Ben E.　　　　A deafness comes to me at times,
　　Born of old age.　I hear your Highness not.

　　　　　　　　　　　　　　　　　　(*Exit.*)

Pret. (*alone*).　As water through the fingers slides, this
　　Jew
　　Escapes me.　Now, my purpose has he probed? . .
　　Should I revoke my word and mew him close
　　Until this enterprise is fairly launched,
　　Lest he attempt to thwart it—warn the Queen,
　　And get the boy removed beyond my reach?
　　A clumsy mode, which might itself defeat. . . .
　　No, I must foil him by a nimbler use
　　Of his own weapons, subtlety and fraud.

　　　　　　　Withold *re-enters.*

Withold.　I hope that when your Highness wears the
　　crown
　　Of this fair realm, your own by right divine,—
Pret.　Not if young Dorion lives.
Wit.　　　　Oh, "if!"　The thought
　　Still haunts you that this stripling whom you saw
　　May be the brother of the Queen, deceased,
　　By all accounts, years since?
Pret.　　　　　　It haunts me still.
　　My uncle's second wife I saw but once,
　　And yet her looks I perfectly recall.

Her name was Alba, and she was indeed
Fair like the dawn.   Conceive, then, my surprise,
During my stolen visit to my love,
When I beheld her breathing picture stand
Before me in the person of a lad—
A lad of eighteen years or thereabout,
The age her son would be if still alive.
But for the male attire I could have sworn
'Twas she herself; the eyes' soft gravity,
Complexion's brilliance, shining hair, superb
Poise of the head, lip's sweet, disdainful curl—
All, all were there, and, as I looked, I thought
Upon the rumour that the child's demise
Was but a fraud.
WIT.   There was such rumour, then?
PRET.   A whisper in the air from time to time,
   Which came, one knew not whence, and died
      away,
   Scarce heeded, so improbable it seemed.
WIT.   Strange.   And the Queen is tender towards this
         lad?
PRET.   Those two wild girls that on the Princess wait
   I questioned, and was led thus much to infer.
WIT.   Should this leak out or ever be revealed
   We must dispute the youth's identity.

PRET.   Nay, we must prove the youth's identity,
   Prove and make known, and that without delay.
WIT.   Proved, it were fatal to your Highness' claim.
PRET.   Listen.   Of my position more and more
   I see the difficulties every day.
   My path lies over steep and dangerous ground.
   Fast as I win one height another soars
   Beyond it, and the goal is yet afar.
   The Queen is young and sweet, a new-made wife,
   And hence the generous sympathies commands
   Of all who by self-interest are not warped ;
   While such as join my standard by their own
   Ambitions or necessities are spurred,
   Far more than by the justice of my cause,
   And nothing but continuous success
   Will hold them faithful.   Yet, could I but prove
   That underneath the semblance of a page
   This Queen of hearts conceals her father's son,
   And wickedly usurps his birthright, love
   To honest indignation I transform,
   With ease displace her from her seat of pride.
   So, through my means, the boy acquires his own ;
   But, being simple, is incompetent
   To govern—in the vehicle of state
   He sits upon the driver's box, but one

Beside him holds the virtual reins of power,—
Is in perpetual nonage, as it were.
He wears of sovereignty the external weeds,
A regent rules.   And who for that proud post
So fit as I, his kinsman, who restored
The lost one to a loving people's arms ;
Who might have won the sceptre for myself,
But so loved right and justice that I gained
Only to place it in the hand august,
Though feeble, of its true inheritor.
WIT.   Then you and your descendants will be mayors
   O' the Palace to a line of sluggard kings ?
PRET.   The lad would never be allowed to wed,
   And found a dynasty of imbeciles :
   The world contains already fools enough.
WIT.   How if he do but feign simplicity ?
PRET.   I fear it not ; I watched him narrowly,
   That know the human countenance to read.
   His nickname designates him truly, mad—
   No, nor yet vicious, only innocent.
   Our cue will be to cause him to appear
   Worse than he is, perchance judiciously
   To irritate him into violence
   Now and again, when such display will tell
   Conveniently against him.   I foresee

That not for long will he demand our care.
Untimely death is written on his cheek.
A few short years, a *very* few, methinks,
And he will slumber in that sepulchre
In which so long ago we thought him laid.
And then, from standing on the topmost step
O' the throne, I slip into the vacant seat,
To which but few will dare dispute my claim.
Thus it is but a temporary change
Of programme, after all, we need to make.

Wit. How shall we get indisputable proof
Of this said stripling's sameness with the Prince
Supposititiously deceased ?

Pret. Ah, there's
The difficulty. Could I win that Jew . . . .
However, know that I have set on foot
Secret investigations, whence I look
For such an issue as shall justify
My project.

Wit. It is needful to obtain
Possession of the person of the youth.

Pret. Undoubtedly.

Wit. And how do you propose
To compass his abduction ?

Pret. How ? You know

I never have recourse to violence
Till stratagem has failed.

WIT.   You nurse some scheme?

PRET. The fairest princess in the world, who means
One day to share a certain throne with me,
To wile the tedium of monotonous days,
And keep her hand in at the game of games
While circumstance divides her from her chosen
Legitimate partner, idly plays at love
With Nardi, the Queen's Innocent. The boy
Is desperately in earnest, as becomes
His eighteen years.

WIT.   In short, you mean to make
A cat's-paw of the Princess.

PRET.   Harshly put.
I mean to make events assume a shape
Shall dove-tail with my purpose.   [*Exeunt.*

SCENE II.—THE SAME AS IN ACT I, SCENE 2.

(SIBYL *and* VERONICA. *Enter the* PRINCESS, *laughing immoderately.*)

PRINCESS. Let me sit down. . . . Oh, I shall die
with mirth!
The Innocent his passion has declared!

VERON. Would I had been in hiding somewhere near,
   For once to witness how a fool makes love !
SIBYL. Oh, all men act the fool when making love.
   You would have witnessed nothing singular.
VERON. And that is true. But did he perpetrate
   Many absurdities? Oh, tell us all !
PRINCESS. His body trembled, and his countenance
   With tears and blushes much disordered grew
   At first, but he became erelong more calm,
   And urged his suit with natural eloquence,
   Though without vehemence. He did not rave.
   His speech was temperate even while his looks
   Were full of fire—whereat I marvelled much,
   That looked for some fantastical display.
SIBYL. Poor soul ; how much I should have pitied him.
PRINCESS. 'Twas pitiful—and yet so laughable !

                              (*laughs again.*)

SIBYL. Well, now the jest is done and I am glad.
   Without undue severity you chid
   This poor young man's presumption ? Did he seem
   Much humbled ?
PRINCESS.   Done ? The jest is but begun.
SIBYL. You surely gave him no encouragement ?
PRINCESS. Poor love would starve without some crumbs
      of hope
   To feed on.

SIBYL.   Better starve at once than live
Hereafter to be strangled by your scorn.
You never gave him leave to cherish hopes,
Hopes—hopes of what ?   You disenchanted him ;
You brushed away the sparkling gossamers
Of this illusion from before his eyes,
With something of remorse for weaving them,
I know you did !

PRINCESS.   And why so soon destroy
What I have been at trouble to create ?
Sententious Sibyl, full of sweet, wise saws,
You check and chide me so I sometimes feel
As if I were a small raw girl of ten,
And you my governess.   Be comforted.
I but divert myself with this young man,
And, rest assured, shall know to pause in time.
Be not so jealous for my honour, dear.

SIBYL.   It is not for your honour that I fear,
Madam, I only pity this poor youth,
Who wooes with so much blended dignity
And passion.

PRINCESS.   This is really excellent.
You were not present with us, I suppose,
When we agreed to make a sport of him ?

SIBYL.   Sport which grows cruel gives me no more joy.

My notion of a jest some limit owns,—
When that is overstepped it is a jest
No longer.   I beseech you, have a care.
You trifle with a demi-lunatic.
The tottering balance of his mind one touch
From you may overturn.

VERON.   Our Sibyl grows
So wondrous tender over this young man !

SIBYL.   He, like the rest, will stumble soon enough
Upon the thorns of life, and bleed, no doubt ;
Then why anticipate and prick his flesh
Out of pure wantonness?   The pangs of love
I wonder has your Highness ever felt ?
No, no, you would not thus so recklessly
Inflict them on another if you had.

PRINCESS (*after a minute's pause*).

Which is the best, to love or be beloved ?
I know which keeps the soul most equable.
Love is at times my guest, at times my slave,
My master never.   Oh, *the pangs of love !*
Our sapient Sibyl speaks from knowledge here.
What are they like, and do they cause the face
To redden and the lip to tremble so ?
That flush becomes her, eh, Veronica ?
The rose upon her cheek 's a thought too pale

At ordinary times. That's better still !

Dear, would you cause those pangs of which you speak,

Look thus. I wish that Aon saw her now !

SIBYL. You do not hurt me, madam.

PRINCESS. You are wrath,

You know it. You may scold and vex and thwart,

And none to vent a murmur must presume ;

But let your fiat be opposed—oh, then

The blood mercurial to your visage flies,

The choler rises in your gorge, as now.

You will not deviate from your own straight course

For aught, but let a craft attempt to cross

Your bows—you run her down without remorse.

You are a little too imperious, yes,—

" Is Lady Sibyl tired ? " The game must cease,

The toy be put away. I do not love

Obsequiousness, 'tis true, but there's a mean

Which you in future would do well to observe.

None but myself shall regulate my acts—

I need no monitress.

Veronica,

Let us go hence and saunter by the lake,

The air is stifling underneath these elms.

(*Exeunt* PRINCESS *and* VERONICA. *They are hardly
gone when the* PRINCE *emerges from the Palace and
descends the steps.*)

PRINCE. I thought to find my sister here.

SIBYL.   They left
   A minute since to go towards the lake,
   She and Veronica.

PRINCE.   I'll follow them.
      (*Is about to go, but pauses, and looks hard at* SIBYL.)
   In tears?

SIBYL.   Oh no!

PRINCE.   You have been weeping?

SIBYL.   No.

PRINCE. It is a clever simulation then.
   Will you not tell an ancient playfellow
   The cause of your distress?

SIBYL.   If know you must,
   The Princess with the freedom of my speech
   Was vexed, and winged to punish me a shaft
   Which feathered she for such occasions keeps—
   A shaft which always wounds. Then I in turn
   Grew angry; but I never can display
   My wrath like others—tears will always come.
   Your Highness now knows all.

PRINCE.   What cause provoked
   The duel, in the course of which you got
   This thrust?

SIBYL.   What cause? A very innocent.

Nardi, the household favourite of the Queen.
We fought about a fool—a foolish strife.

PRINCE.   A foolish strife indeed.   I wonder much
What ladies see worth crossing swords about
In such a milksop.

SIBYL.   You are jealous ; fie !

PRINCE.   An idle, insolent, presumptuous boy,
That should be whipped, and set to learn some trade.

SIBYL.   Have you conceived a grudge against the lad ?

PRINCE.   A   shrill-tongued,   baby-faced,   effeminate
thing,—
You women would do just as well to pet
A slip of your own sex.   His garments' cut
Is the sole part about him masculine.
I half believe he is a girl disguised.

SIBYL.   Wait till he gets a beard, and you will see.

PRINCE.   No chin of his will ever wear a beard.

SIBYL.   Has he informed your Highness he intends
To go smooth-shaven always ?

PRINCE.   You may laugh—
But his contemptible bulk has come this day
Between the Queen and me, and caused eclipse.

SIBYL.   Partial, of course.

PRINCE.   Not total, you may guess.

SIBYL.   But how ?

PRINCE.   I found him with the Queen alone,
Seated upon a level with her feet.
He rose and moved aside, but did not leave
The presence as I entered ; so I said
He might withdraw.   He looked me in the face,
But stood.   I spoke again, peremptorily.
He stared, but never stirred.   This insolence
So tried me, I was minded sore to take
The measure of his shoulders with my cane,
But only said that I would summon one
Who should by force remove him.   Thereupon
He straightway, like a monkey in a pet,
With face convulsed and inarticulate cries,
Flew to the Queen.   She chid him, it is true,
But in such soothing tones as robbed the words
Of all reproof.   Then Master Malapert
Laid his scorched cheek a moment on her hand,
And darted from the room.

SIBYL.   The wisest thing
That he could do.   .

PRINCE.   But that which vexed me most
Was, that the Queen, the moment he was gone,
Should warmly take his part.   He meant no harm,
She said, no rudeness, and was quite unused
To bear rebuke from any but herself.

SIBYL. I like her Majesty, I do indeed,
For championing her favourite.

PRINCE. Sibyl!

SIBYL. Yes,
Had I been she I would have done the same.
Look yonder—they perceive and beckon you.

PRINCE (*going*). But would you not such championship
resent,
Were you the husband of her Majesty?

SIBYL (*looking round as she ascends the steps of the Palace*)
The husband?—Oh, a husband is a mute
Enduring thing, obedient to the rein.
It jibbs, and champs the bit a little at first,
But after it is fully broken in—

PRINCE. Oh, this is treason!—I will hear no more.
[*Exit.*

SCENE III.—A ROOM IN THE PALACE. THE *Queen*,
Nardi, AND *Ben Ephraim.*

NARDI. But, madam, I maintain there should not be
Such splendour and such squalor side by side.
You say a human being has a soul,
And brutes have none ; yet here are human beings,
Within a stone's throw of the Palace gate,
Worse lodged and scantlier nourished than your hounds.

QUEEN. Why am I thus arraigned? Can I abolish
　　Vice and improvidence? If these are poor—
　　Good cause; you say the father is a sot.
　　The children suffer for the parents' sins
　　In other ranks of life besides the lowest.

NARDI. I saw the sky in places through the roof;
　　The floor is nothing but the trodden earth—
　　Not even flagged. And she is—oh, so thin!
　　She scarce gets nourishment enough to keep
　　Her body and soul from parting company.
　　And this is all within one little mile
　　Of where you sit beneath a painted ceiling,
　　And diet on the daintiest meats, served up
　　On golden dishes. And her bones are racked—
　　Her poor misshapen bones—with cruel pains,
　　Contracted through the damps. I only wish
　　Your Majesty both her and her abode
　　Could see.

QUEEN. 　　　　I thank you—I would rather not.

NARDI. She is so young—a child—not yet fifteen.
　　They say that God is good, and we are all
　　His children, and He loves us all alike.
　　I cannot think it when I see His gifts
　　So partially distributed—that some
　　Have all and others none; if I were He——

QUEEN. I will not hear impiety. Leave God
  Out of your talk. You lack religion, Nardi.
NARDI (*passionately*). Well, then, if I were king, as you
    are queen,
  I would not dress until the poor were clothed!
  I would not eat until the poor were fed!
  Why, I would sell the jewels in the crown ——
QUEEN. Stop! There's my purse. (*Throwing it on
    the table*). Relieve these people's wants.
  And buy a bridle for your tongue, moreover,
  It grows unruly.
NARDI.   Madam,——
QUEEN.   No more words.
  Too many are said already. You abuse
  The license I allow you of free speech.
  Begone, and do not meet my sight again
  This day.
            (NARDI *snatches up the purse and vanishes.*)
            His tongue is sharper than a sword!
  Ben Ephraim, ascertain if all he says
  Of their extreme necessity be true.
  Now to return—he really bears such strong
  Resemblance to his mother? Time has blurred
  Her picture in my mind.
BEN E.   He has her hair,

And her complexion, and his lip, I note,
Will curl like hers when something angers him
Or moves his scorn.   But kin-resemblances
Are very fleeting and capricious.   Oft
A stranger catches them, whenas they elude
The more familiar.   'Neath the stress at times
Of sudden strong emotion, forth they flash,
Are chiselled out by lengthened physical pain,
Or take possession of the face at death.
At times 'tis some hereditary quaint
Trick of expression that will call to mind
Another individual of the race.
Few are less like than you and he, yet once,
Entering his chamber while he slept, I saw
The strangest momentary similitude.

QUEEN.   Would he had never seen the Court!

BEN E.   That wish
I echo.

QUEEN.   And in echoing it imply
A sharp reproof.   In placing him so near
Our royal person we did act, we know,
In opposition to your sage advice.
'Tis true you warned us, and we would not heed.
We now repent, and own ourselves to blame.

                    (*Paces the stage in thought.*)
The Count was very civil to you, then?

BEN E. Most smooth and courteous, all the while he
    sought
  To fathom with his delicate plummet line
  My depths.

QUEEN.   Where undercurrents flowed, I hope,
  So strong they bore his lead up like a cork.
  What use of this discovery will he make?
  How if he hold the secret in reserve,
  And, when he finds his own a hopeless cause,
  Espouses that of Dorion? I will fight
  Against this rebel villain cousin of mine
  While I've a soldier left, but raise no hand
  Against my father's son ; should he demand
  His birthright I would yield it him at once,
  Yes, give him up the crown, and only pray
  It prove less thorny to his brows than mine.
  Oh, I have half a mind to call the peers,
  Before them Nardi set, and all the truth
  Reveal; and thus the worst anticipate,
  And cut the knot of my perplexities
  Once and for ever !

BEN E.   Madam, such an act
  Would tangle your perplexities the more.
  Untie the burden from your neck, because
  It chafes you somewhat and is hard to bear,

F

And hang it upon Nardi's, which would sink
Beneath it in a day?   Fie, madam, fie !
A petulant girl spoke then and not the Queen.

QUEEN.   You are outspoken and severe, and yet
So true a servant I must needs forgive.
What has your wisdom to suggest?

BEN E.   But this—
That Nardi to some distant secret place
Of safety should be sent without delay.

QUEEN.   His sudden disappearance would beget
Surmises, which might easily become
Suspicions.

BEN E.   If the tale we fabricate
To lend a natural colour to his going
Have likelihood, I see not why it need.

QUEEN.   More fictions?   Well, arrange it as you please.
We hold you answerable for his life
And safety always.

                              [*Exeunt.*

SCENE 4.—A VILLAGE STREET.

*Enter, from opposite sides, TIMOTHY clattering his pots
and pans, and MORRA.*

MORRA.   Folks say that grandf'er can't live out the night.

TIM.   I've done my duty by him, that is clear.
And I shall put the old man underground
With a clean conscience.   Anybody else
Had sent him to the workhouse long ago.
Your mother's father—that was all he was.
Well, we must all die somewhen, I suppose.
What do you cry for?   'Tis but an old man,
And childish. . . .   Look you now, if it were me,
If it were me now—a good father, Morra,
Ay, though I say it.   When your mother died
I was a comely man—ay, that I was !
Many's the lass that would have had me then.
But no, says I, no, no, there's little Morra,
There's Morra and the old one now to work for,—
MORRA.   I'm most afeared to be alone with him,
His eyes do get to look so wild and strange.
TIM.   Afeared !—his eyes can't do you any harm.
What is it you are hiding in your breast ?
Has that young gallant been to you again ?
Ah, and he gave you something, I'll be bound.
Hand it to me to keep for you, d'ye hear ?
What do young lasses know of money's worth ?
A purse of gold, as I'm a Christian man !
Let go, I say, ye disobedient minx !

(Tears it out of her hand.)

F 2

MORRA.   The money was to get the roof new thatched,
    To keep the wet out—and to have the place
    Boarded and made more decent—and to buy
    Physic and food for grandf'er, and—and now—(*sobs.*)
TIM.   There, leave off snivelling.   I shall keep it safe.
                    (*Jingles the money against his ear.*)
MORRA.   Give me the money back.   The money's
    mine.
TIM.   A likely story.   Yours !   Who's found your keep
    These fourteen years, I'd like to know, and held
    A roof above your head ? you thankless toad !
    You crook-backed—
MORRA.   Don't I know that you will never
    Be sober any more until it's gone ?—
    The money that was meant to do us good,
    That are so poor !
TIM.   There, you be off ! go home !
    I shall keep sober.
MORRA.   You ! the drunkenest man
    In all the parish !   While the money lasts
    You'll do no work, but drink and lie about.
    They say, folks do, you ought to be ashamed—
TIM.   You viper, you !   Take that—and that—
    (*beats her with his stick*) and learn
    What's owing to a parent.
                    (MORRA *runs off, screaming.*)

SCENE 5.—LAWN BY THE SIDE OF AN ARTIFICIAL LAKE.
MOONLIGHT.

Enter NARDI, *with his guitar, and the* PRINCESS.

NARDI.   I knew you years before we met.   I thought
  That death and you were one thing and the same.
PRINCESS.   How so?
NARDI.   As long as I can recollect,
  A shadowy, shrouded shape has haunted me,
  The vision of, as 'twere, a human form,
  But draped from head to foot.   None ever saw
  This thing beside, though I beheld it oft
  With others by.   I used to think that death
  Was underneath the veil, and if it once
  Began to lift, my sand would soon be run.
  At length one night while broad awake I lay,
  A voice, that voice which tells me everything,
  Said in my ear, "The veil is lifted—see!"
  I looked, and "Death is very fair," I thought,
  "Death is an angel after all."   Next day—
  A wonder! for I saw your face, and lo,
  My vision in the flesh!   Strange pain, and joy
  Still stranger seized me then.   "But this is life,
  Not death!" I murmured, for indeed it seemed
  I had not truly waked to life till then.
  Slumber the following night my pillow shunned,

But when the sky was growing flushed with dawn
I rose, and knelt, and wildly clasped my hands,
And " Is it life or death ? " with streaming eyes
I cried.   The voice of which I spoke before
Then answered, " Neither—yet the cause of both."
PRINCESS.   What meant the voice by that—" the cause
    of both ?"
I do not understand these parables.
You are too fine and spiritual for me.
Sing me a song that I can comprehend.
(Sits down on a garden-seat.   NARDI places himself be-
    side her and tunes his guitar.)

NARDI *(sings).*

    A Brave of some Red Indian tribe were you—
      Mohawk or Blackfoot, Blood, or Snake, or Sioux,—
    And I a dusky maiden of the same ;
      My father's weapons I should steal, beside
      Some forest trail that you must follow hide,
    And, as with stately step along you came,
    An arrow tipped with death at your brown bosom aim.

PRINCESS.   Oh, what a savage song !   Who made it ?
NARDI.   I,
    When in a savage mood.

PRINCESS. But what know you
About Red Indians?

NARDI. What I find in books.
There's one about them in the library—
With pictures in it—which I often read.
I'll show it you some day.

> *(Continues his song, with a change of measure.)*

My heart would feel as light as air
  As soon as yours had ceased to beat,
    And once again the heavens would smile,
    And, for at least a little while,
  The flowers smell sweet,
The stars look fair.

Your brother Braves would find you cold ;
  And all my jealous fears might cease,
    And all the passion, pain, and strife
    That you have brought into my life,—
  With you at peace
Beneath the mould.

PRINCESS *(after a pause)*. Then you have loved
Before?

NARDI. Oh, 1 have always loved, but you
Have been the single star of my desire,
Sole beacon of my hope.

PRINCESS.   You strangest boy ! . . .
How hot the evening grows—let go my hand !
(*Rises abruptly and moves to the other side of the stage.*
NARDI follows her half-way, then pauses and sings
the following.)

Sweet air, sweet rain, the glowing soft caress
Of June's rich sunshine—these the rose demands,
These, ere from bud to blossom it expands ;
    My heart is such a rose, and asks no less,
Before it can unfurl its petals frail,
And such poor perfume as they shroud exhale.

What sumptuous June is to the garden's queen,
That Love is to my heart, which 'neath your smile
Thrills, kindles, and uncloses,—this long while
    Love but a plainer name for you has been,—
Your tears sweet rain, your kisses are sweet air ;
The flower you fostered take—ah, take and wear !

(*Approaches and possesses himself of her hand once more.*)

Dear angel, we will marry without delay.
Though you are such a great and proud princess,
. And I am nothing in the world's esteem,
    Love makes us equal.   I shall go and kneel

Low at the sovereign's feet, and tell her all.
The Queen is kind, and holds me somewhat dear,
And when she learns our hearts are wholly set
On one the other, she will not withhold
This coveted hand.

PRINCESS.   I never knew the Queen
Had power to give or to withhold my hand.
You must be patient and leave all to me.
And see you do not breathe a word of this
To any, if you do—that very hour
You forfeit my regard.   Now go and tell
My ladies to rejoin me.

(NARDI *departs reluctantly. The* PRINCESS *looks after
him.*)

                 This young man
Gets vehement.   I grow afraid of him.
If he should go and babble to the Queen—
Saints, what a coil there'd be !   The jest must end.

                         [*Exit.*

ACT III.

SCENE I.—CURTAIN RISES TO MUSIC, AND DISCOVERS A RICHLY DECORATED HALL FILLED WITH DANCERS. THE MUSIC CEASES AND THE DANCERS PROMENADE. SUDDENLY THE THRONG DIVIDES, AND THE *Queen*, CONVERSING WITH A MILITARY OFFICER OF RANK, AND ATTENDED BY A BRILLIANT COMPANY, PASSES DOWN THE MIDDLE OF THE STAGE.

QUEEN.   I marvel much your losses should have been
So slight.
OFFICER.   Your Majesty must understand
Our shrapnels, in the first place, had upon
The rebels told with terrible success,
Lessening their numbers and their courage both,
Before the storming actually began.
And in the second place the hill itself
Was too precipitous to let them fire
Over the earthworks with the best effect.
Most of their rifle shots were aimed too high.
The inside of the last redoubt, which all
The natural platform of the hill comprised,
Was ploughed by shells and with their fragments
    strewn.
        (*The* PRINCE *enters.*)

PRINCE.   My Gladys, you have danced but once to-
night.

QUEEN.   I do not feel to-night in dancing mood.
To hear the storming of the three redoubts
Described in detail interests me more.
But do not you on that account refrain.
The Lady Sibyl lacks a partner.   Go.

[Exit the PRINCE.

OFFICER.   His Highness is a famous dancer.

QUEEN.   Yes.
To dance affords him a most keen delight.

(Exeunt.   The PRINCESS *and a* CAVALIER *emerge from
the background.* VERONICA *and another at the same
time enter at the side.   The couples meet, and* VERO-
NICA *draws the* PRINCESS *apart.)*

VERONICA.   Some hand in mine just now, as through
the crowd
Of pages and of servitors I passed,
This paper slipped.   It's meant for you, I judge.

PRINCESS.   Pharamond's writing !   Shield me while I read.

(Reads.)

" I would have speech with you upon a thing
Of moment ; wherefore seek with all despatch,
Caution, and secrecy, the haunted grot."
The haunted grot ?

VERON.   I know.   One afternoon
  Sibyl and I, out walking by ourselves,
  Took shelter in it from a shower of rain.
  It is a curious hollow in the hill,
  That hill whose dark green crest you sometimes chide,
  When looking westward from our balcony,
  Because it interposes to conceal
  The point of sunset.   Nardi afterwards
  Told us its name.
PRINCESS.   And should you find the way?
VERON.   If we could slip out unperceived I might.
PRINCESS.   I wonder is the moon risen?
VERON.   Scarcely yet.
  At all events, the sky is packed with clouds.
  But seriously you do not meditate
  Obeying this strange mandate?
PRINCESS.   Wherefore not?
VERON.   'Tis madness! We shall catch our deaths of
      cold ;
  Though that's no matter.   But the way is long
  And lonesome—horribly, by daylight even,
  By night—
PRINCESS.   This grot is haunted then, they say?
VERON.   Yes, and the ghost is palpable it seems.

  (*Cavaliers rejoin them. More dancing. The* PRINCE
and SIBYL *enter.*)

PRINCE. The doctor rules her head, the fool her heart.
  A precious pair.

SIBYL.   Well, now the fool is gone.

PRINCE. Yes, gone ; and whither has he gone, and
    where ?

SIBYL. 'Tis said that on a sudden, two days since,
  He overpassed that shadowy border line,
  Upon the hither side of which he seemed
  So long to hover,—that his wits and he
  Have definitely parted company.

PRINCE. A fiction. He is spirited away,
  Because she saw that he had grown to me
  An object of suspicion and dislike,
  To some retreat in which their mutual—

SIBYL.   Sir—
  Mutual? Well, there at least you are deceived.
  You think that Nardi loves the Queen. His heart
  Is fixed elsewhere. It is the Princess—

PRINCE.   Ha !—
  He loves my sister ? Now I see it all !
  I see,—the Queen has snatched him from the toils
  Of her enchanting rival !

SIBYL.   Be it so.
  I will not argue with a man so bent
  On being jealous. If you like the rack,

Pray lie on it. 'Twould serve you right to give
The engine a gratuitous turn or two.

PRINCE. 'Tis clear she does not love me. Who should share
Her secret counsels if not I, her lord?
And where should perfect confidence exist
If not 'twixt man and wife, who grew, I thought,
One soul as well as flesh?—Yet we are twain,
And every day divides us more and more.

SIBYL. This ere the honeymoon be spent? Poor Prince!

PRINCE. I seem but like a guest within the home
Which rightly I am head of; while the Jew
Is daily closeted alone with her,
And holds the key of that locked treasury,
Her bosom. Yet the greybeard I could brook.
It is the boy—the boy that maddens me!

SIBYL. The reason of her partiality
For Nardi why not bluntly ask?

PRINCE.   I did.
I questioned her about his parentage,
And how he chanced to come to be at Court,
And why she chose to make so much of him.
The Princess joined us ere she could reply,
And so no more was said; but since that hour

She ever seems to stand upon her guard,
And does not care to be alone with me
More than she well can help.   And now the youth
Has vanished—whither is vouchsafed to none.

SIBYL (*after a pause*).

There's more in this than on the surface shows.
I think if I were in your Highness' place,
Husband to such a lady as the Queen,
I know what I would do.

PRINCE.   What would you do?

SIBYL.   Shame her by having confidence in her;
Bear with her patiently, and think no ill.
This modest counsel will you deign to take
From one who dares to call herself your friend?

PRINCE.   Sibyl, I know not—

SIBYL.   See, her Majesty
Approaches.   It is supper, I expect.

Re-enter the QUEEN, *attended.   She smiles and holds
out her hand to the* PRINCE.

                [*Exeunt all.*

SCENE 2.   NIGHT.   BROKEN GROUND AT THE FOOT OF
A HILL, WELL WOODED ROUND ABOUT.   TO THE RIGHT,
PARTLY CONCEALED BY A YOUNG TREE WHICH HAS
GROWN UP ATHWART IT, THE MOUTH OF A GROTTO,
FROM WHICH EMERGE THE *Pretender* AND *Withold.*

WIT.   How if the Princess be incompetent
  Your summons to obey?

PRET.   Tsh! man—she'll come.

WIT.   Or if, attending it, she yet refuse
  This stripling to betray.

PRET.   She'll not refuse.
  The business is a ticklish one, I know.
  But if this card is to be played at all,
  'Tis certain I must hold it in my hand
  Ere noon to-morrow.   Hark! was that a step?
  Begone.   And have a care you do not miss
  The path—the second to your left—the felled
  Timber will be your guide.   The men prepared
  For any hazard or contingence keep.

  (*Exit* WITHOLD.   *The* PRETENDER *retires into the
    grotto.   Enter the* PRINCESS *and* VERONICA, *closely
    wrapped.*)

PRINCESS.   Not near it yet?

VERON.   It must be hereabout.

  (*The* PRETENDER *is in the act of coming forth when*
    NARDI, *suddenly darting into view round a spur of the
    hill, leaps on to the stage immediately in front of the
    two ladies.*)

VERON. (*clinging to the Princess*).
  Have mercy on us!   He has broken loose,

And comes to murder us, as like as not.

Stark mad he is—I see it in his eye !

NARDI. I did not mean to startle you so much.

I am as sane as you. Here, feel how calm

My pulses beat—

(*Extends his wrist to* VERONICA, *and presses the reluct-
ant hand of the* PRINCESS *against his heart.*)

       although small marvel 'twere

If, after three long arctic-winter days

Unwarmed by any ray your presence sheds,

This meeting made them galop.

PRINCESS.   You were fallen

Into a dangerous frenzy which required

Your transfer to a madhouse, it was said.

NARDI. If I am mad, then all mankind is mad.

PRINCESS. 'Twas falsehood, then, about your being
    removed ?

But where have you been hidden these three days ?

NARDI. It is a fact that I was forced away,

Though what my destination was to be

I know not. Happily I 'scaped my guards.

VERON. You hear—he is a lunatic at large.

I knew he was,—I said so,—

PRINCESS.   Peace, you fool !

G

Run to the thicket and keep watch, that none
Surprise us.
            [*Exit* VERONICA *with reluctance.*
(*To* NARDI.)   Now this mystery explain.
The whole that has befallen you relate.

NARDI.   A prisoner in my chamber I was kept
For two whole days ; the third (to-day), at dawn,
Doctor Ben Ephraim stood beside my bed,
And bade me rise and preparation make
To go upon a journey which the Queen
Willed I should undertake.   I, wondering, asked,
" Whither ? "   He answered, " Later you shall learn."
" Shall I return to-day ? "   " No, not to-day."
" To-morrow ? "   " Nor to-morrow."   In dismay,
" This journey then means banishment," I cried.
" For what offence must I be exiled thus ? "
" For none."   " Why go, then ? "   " 'Tis the Queen's
      command."
Then seeing I began my hands to wring,
" Have you not ever found the Queen," he said,
" A gentle mistress ? "   I agreed.   " Then yield
Unquestioning obedience to her now.
Here is a parting gift she sends you—read
The motto."   And, with that, an antique ring
He handed to me which I oft have marked

Upon the finger of the Queen, inscribed
With " *Trust me and be patient.*"   Here it is.
I dressed myself with such a heavy heart !
Six months ago I had not cared a bit,
One place was like another then, but now
Exile from Court meant banishment from you.
The Queen had learnt the secret of our love,
And meant to part us, that I plainly saw.

PRINCESS.   You really think this journey was designed
For such an end ?

NARDI.   I rack my mind in vain
To hit on any other it could have.

PRINCESS.   You think you—we have been discovered,
then ?
That our—that your——continue with your tale.

NARDI.   When every pretext for delay was spent,
I bade my chamber silent, sad farewell,
And traversed, by that old physician's side,
The quiet palace.   At the postern gate
There stood a coach, and near it two strange men,
On seeing whom I straight drew back and cried,
" These two are jailers—no, I will not go ! "
Then, at a sign, that pair laid hold on me
And forced me in, and off at once we drove.
I soon was lost in sorrowful thought, and took

Small note of time or of the way we went ;
But suddenly I woke to a confused
Sensation of alarm.   We then had just
Rounded the shoulder of a hill, the air
Felt dense and sultry, and a gloom as deep
Almost as that of night o'erhung the scene.
A minute more, however, and a flash
The vividest I ever witnessed clove
The darkness, followed instantly by one
Long, solitary, deafening thunder peal.
The men inside the coach with me looked pale ;
I laughed hysterically and clapped my hands.
The horses at the same time reared with fright,
Then started off and, at a furious pace,
Went tearing madly down the steep incline.
Before my guards could know of my intent,
I oped the carriage door and out I leapt.
The tumble stunned me, but the splashing rain
That poured upon my face revived me soon,
And up from off the ground I rose unhurt,
Barring some bruises and a shoulder sprain.
One of my guards lay sprawling on his back
Upon the turf some few yards off, stone dead.
Of coach, or driver, or the other guard—
No sign.   I laid the dead man straight, and crossed

His wrists, and spread a kerchief on his face.
I then walked back along the road we came.
Sunshine succeeded storm.   I walked for hours,
Or so it seemed, and never met a soul.
At length I reached the outskirts of the woods,
And soon sharp strokes, as of a woodman's axe,
Smote on my ear.   I hastened towards the noise,
And found a friendly peasant whom I knew,
Who took me to his hut, and gave me food,
And dried my clothes ; and there I lay concealed
Till evening cast her mantle on the land.

PRINCESS.   What next do you propose to do?   Ere
    now,
News must have reached the Queen of your escape,
And searchers, it is likeliest, are abroad.

NARDI.   You are a timely riser, walking forth
    Most mornings with your ladies,—one of those
    To whom the beauty of the matin star
    Is not a thing unknown, nor how divine
    The savour is of lichen-traceried pines,
    When winds at dawning sough amid their tops.

PRINCESS.   And what of that?

NARDI.   At dawn to-morrow rise,
    And seek that triad of gigantic elms

Which marks the limit of the forest free—
"The Sisters," it is called—you know the spot.
There shall you meet a peasant girl deformed,
A little witch-like figure, follow her,
And she will guide you to a chapel small,
Veiled in thick woodland shades.   Within its walls
I, with a priest, your coming will await.
The nuptial blessing fast pronounced, we two
Will walk into the presence of the Queen,
And tell her what irrevocable thing
Has taken place between us, and abide
Her pleasure.

(*The* PRINCESS, *having recovered from her first astonishment, has a strong inclination to laugh, but checks it.*)

PRINCESS.   Oh !—you take me by surprise.
Where is the need of such precipitate haste ?

NARDI.   The wild-horse, opportunity, is caught
Seldom a second time ; for these few hours,
Only these few, he stands at our command,
And, if we boldly leap upon his back,
Will bear us to the goal of our desire.
You hesitate . . . I fear then, after all,
You do not care for me.

PRINCESS.   'Twould ill become
A woman other than to hesitate

At such a crisis ; ere I can decide
I must have leisure to deliberate.

NARDI.   At stroke of midnight one whom I can trust
Shall underneath your chamber-window stand.
Indite the "yea" or "nay" which is to bless
Or damn me, and despatch it through the air.

PRINCESS.   Midnight—'tis ten o'clock already—well,
It shall be done.

NARDI.   You love me ?

PRINCESS.   Doubt it not.

NARDI.   Then why not say at once that you agree
To my proposal ?

PRINCESS.   Hush ! I hear a sound.

NARDI.   It is the wind.

PRINCESS.   There's not a breath astir.

NARDI.   It is a bird that roosts among the boughs.
You are not paltering with me, are you ?   Come—
Before we separate I'll seal my fate.

> (*Grasps both her hands in his.*)

Swear you will meet and wed with me at morn !

PRINCESS.   Leave go !

> (*Struggles to free herself.   Screams.   The* PRETENDER
> *springs out of his place of concealment on one side,*
> VERONICA *rushes in on the other.*)

VERON.   What is it ?   Nardi, come away !
Someone approaches—quick !

NARDI (*as he is being dragged off by* VERONICA).
                At midnight, then !

(*The* PRETENDER *regards the* PRINCESS *sternly for
some seconds ; then lifts and scans successively her
hands.*)

PRINCESS.   What are you looking for ?

PRET.   My mother's ring.
I placed it on your finger on that day
Which saw us secretly betrothed.

PRIN.   'Tis here,—
Warm at my heart.
                (*Drawing a riband from her neck.*)

PRET.   I want it.   Give it me . . .
A bond that binds so slackly may as well
Be loosened altogether.   You are free.

PRIN.   Are you so angry ?

PRET.   Have I cause or no ? . . .
To-morrow is it ?   Well, I wish him joy.
The Queen will bless and pardon both, no doubt.

PRINCESS.   The Queen, right well you know, will have
no cause
To bless or pardon either.

PRET.   Oh, for shame !—
  Where is the dignity, the high reserve,
  That like a garment should a princess wrap,—
  Should 'twixt the meaner sort and her erect
  A barrier viewless but impassable,
  Which paralyses every foot not royal
  That tries its line to cross?   It makes me blush,
  Thus from yourself to see you derogate—
  Forget your royalty.

PRINCESS.   When next I hear
  The term *unblushing* mated with your name,
  I shall feel glad to know it undeserved.

PRET.   A youth like that to dare lay hands on you,
  And talk of love and marriage—'tis too much !
  Yet there's a modest look about his face . . .
  It needed warm encouragement from you
  To breed such boldness in him, I'll be sworn.

PRINCESS.   How if I were to call you to account
  For every trifling act of gallantry ?
  Oh, there come whispers floating in the air,
  Which often, were my ear unwise enough
  To harbour them, might cause me jealous throes !

PRET.   Throes groundless then . . .
                              But come, 'tis best we part.

I wish him joy who weds a light coquette,
That will not I.

        (*He turns to go.*)

PRINCESS (*catching him by the sleeve*).

      Shall one so mean create
Dissension between princes? You might feel
As reasonably jealous of the dog
That gambols round me and my foot impedes,
The kitten that I nurse, the instrument
From which I draw sweet sounds in idle hours.
What is he after all? A brain-sick boy,
Not yet nineteen, and younger than his years.
I let him sing to me, and hold my fan,
And walk beside me whilst I took the air ;
And when the fool conceived himself in love,
Just for pure sport forebore to check his flame.
We owe our lives to him, my girls and I—
We three must here have yawned ourselves to death
But for this Nardi, whose ingenuousness
Yielded us food for mirth. That now the joke
Becomes a little serious I admit,
But here, I vow, it ends. I never dreamed
That you would view it in so grave a light.

PRET. You never dreamed I should discover it.

PRINCESS.   That I so deeply have offended you,
   I grieve most truly.   Do you pardon me?
PRET.   Give me a kiss.
PRINCESS.   Now hand me back my ring.
PRET.   Inform me first, with reference to this youth,
   How you propose to act, to be exempt
   From further importunities?
PRINCESS.   How act?—
   Oh, make the Queen aware her truant dove
   Is hovering hereabout.   Instruct her how.
   Her birdcatchers may lime him in the woods
   To-morrow morn, perhaps.   His Innocence
   Shall rue, I warrant him, my recent fright.
   See the red mark his sacrilegious grasp
   Has left upon my wrist . . . it tingles still.
PRET.   Will you be ruled in this affair by me?
PRINCESS.   Yea, if your rule be wiser than mine own.
PRET.   Then send him notice, by the appointed means,
   Your coy reluctance to his ardour yields,
   And, two hours after dawn, you will not fail
   To meet him at the sacred spot he named.
PRINCESS (*with a soft laugh of approval*).
   Oh, yes—what else?
PRET.   I undertake the rest.
PRINCESS.   Be more explicit.

Pret. Say there is a child,
The soundness of whose limbs to me is dear.
One day I find it playing with a knife,
And, trembling for its fingers, I demand
The dangerous implement. The little one,
If good, will yield it up to me at once.
You see the drift of my small parable?

Princess. What will you do with this sharp instrument?

Pret. Encase it with a purple velvet sheath,
And make it impotent henceforth to harm.

Princess. What does that mean—*a purple velvet
sheath?*
To sheathe must signify to imprison.

Pret. No;
I take a genuine interest in the boy,
And shall promote his welfare in a way
That will surprise you.

Princess. Must I really, then,
Into your hands "The Innocent" betray?

Pret. Would you this bauble which I hold in pledge,
And what it is a symbol of, redeem.
'Tis after all but yielding me, you know,
Your kitten or your terrier.

PRINCESS. You are not
Bloody or vengeful that I know of, yet—
Did I suspect you meant to kill or hurt
My kitten or my terrier, I might pause
Before I placed it thus within your power.
Give me your word that Nardi shall remain
Unscathed in life and limb.

PRET. Most willingly.
Upon my honour he shall not be harmed.

PRINCESS. They say that you are perjured, and have none
To swear by.

PRET. Well, then, by our love—

PRINCESS. They say
That love and policy with you are one!

PRET. Then by your heavenly beauty, which should be
A warrant for my love,—

PRINCESS. They say that none
Can flatter women like the Count of Ghyl!

PRET. Enough of what they say. The question is,
Will my Cleodora do the thing I ask?

PRINCESS. Well, I shall let you take him off my hands.

PRET. You promise?

PRINCESS. Yes, I promise. Now, my ring.
But, Pharamond, to think that you should thus
Be jealous!—

VERONICA *re-enters.*

VERON.   Will your Highness now return?
  The clouds are breaking, we shall not go back
  Shadowless as we came, but mid a glare
  Of tell-tale moonlight, if we longer stay.

PRINCESS.   What sound is that?

VERON.   The barking of a dog.
  It grows more near.   .   .   The rangers are abroad.

PRET.   No soul will venture here at such an hour,
  The grot too sick a reputation bears.
  Nevertheless, Veronica is right,
  You two had best return.

PRINCESS.   And all this while
  You have not told me why you sent for me!

PRET.   'Tis very true.   And there is now no time
  To remedy the omission.   See! the moon.
  Hie back with caution and your nimblest speed.
  We must contrive, ere long, to meet again.

(*They hurriedly salute and part.*)

PRET. (*alone*).   My plan was nebulous an hour ago,
  Now it is definite, resolved, and clear.
  'Tis ever best when things arrange themselves.

(*Exit.*)

SCENE 3.—INTERIOR OF A SQUALID HUT.
The INNOCENT *and* MORRA.

MORRA. But are there not more gods than one in
heaven?

NARDI. Eh?—only God the Father and His Son.
There is the devil—but he lives in hell.

MORRA. Does he make boys and girls, as well as God?

NARDI. No, only God—He makes, and the devil mars.

MORRA. Perhaps He made me straight and white like
you ;
And then the devil bent me out of shape,
And scorched me brown, and spoiled me.   I would
kill
The devil if I were God!

NARDI.   Perhaps He can't.
Life and the world is all a mystery.
It crushes me to think of it at times !
Some say 'tis all a phantasm.

MORRA.   What is that?

NARDI. A thing unreal, a show.   When I hear sounds
That others do not hear, and gaze on shapes
Lovely or terrible where others see
Nothing but empty space, they say that these

Are phantasms—hollow semblances that only
Live in the mind by which they are perceived.

MORRA (*after a pause*).
   The wrinkles all went out of grandfer's face
   When he was dead.

NARDI.   No doubt.

                    (*Sings in a dreamy sort of chant.*) ·

      Death's damp touch at once effaces
         What life's busy hand has written ;
         Where the soul was speared or smitten,
      Now of wound or bruise no traces ;
         Fold and wrinkle disappear,
         All is once more smooth and clear.

MORRA.   I always cry
   To hear you sing, and yet it makes me feel
   So happy !

NARDI.   Little Morra, I shall tell
   The Princess to befriend you for my sake.
   And you shall have good clothes, and proper food,
   And medicines to ease your bones of pain ;
   And wheresoever we may chance to dwell,
   There shall your home be.

MORRA.   How am I to know
   The Princess from her maids ?

NARDI.   You will not see
Her maids when she is by.   The eye takes in
Nothing but her.

MORRA.   I do so long, yet fear
To see her.   Is her hair all gold like yours?

NARDI.   Yes, gold, but warmer, ruddier—oh, such hair!
It seems to weigh her head back when she walks,—
Dark if she sits in shade, but in the sun
A thousand flames seem flickering in and out
Among its little billows.

                    (*He goes to the window.*)
                    Morra, look!
There's the first streak of dawn—oh, joy!—and there
The morning star—how silver-fair it shines!
The sky grows red.   My bridal morn, all hail!

                    (*He moves towards the door.*)

MORRA.   Where are you going?—to the chapel?

NARDI.   Yes.

MORRA.   Why do you go so soon?

NARDI.   I want to deck
The altar, before which we are to kneel,
With boughs and wild flowers.   You will not mistake,
Morra, the time at which you are to meet
The Princess?

MORRA.   No, oh no, I'll not mistake.

                                                    ^

NARDI (*singing as he goes out into the dawn*).

> Hail to my bridal morning !
> Hail, planet fair, adorning
> The rosy brow of day—ah, day divine for me !
> The music's jar is ended,
> The discord long suspended
> Resolves—my life grows one victorious harmony !
> Rise, sun, and star, wax pale,
> My spousal morning, hail !

> Hail to my bridal morning !
> Hail, beam that gives me warning
> 'T is near—the hour for which I pant with fond desire !
> I feel my stature growing ;
> I feel my breast o'erflowing ;
> My pulses bound, my blood is changed to liquid fire !
> Rise, sun, and star, wax pale,
> My spousal morning, hail !

SCENE 4.—AN APARTMENT IN THE PALACE.

(*Enter the* PRINCESS, SIBYL, *and* VERONICA.)

VERON.   No one here ?
Do you not wonder, Princess, why the Queen
Has summoned us ?

PRINCESS.   I never wonder.

(*Sinks indolently into a chair.*)

Oh!

SIBYL.   Your shoulder pains you?

PRINCESS.   Every time I move.

I must have taken cold in it last night.

VERON.   How does the would-be bridegroom feel by
     now?

To think you might this day have been a wife!

(*Sings.*)

Oh, if I had only said "yea,"
Instead of that foolish word "nay,"
I might have been married to-day!

The youth who was eager to wed me,
This morn to the altar had led me—

PRINCESS.   For heaven's sake, hush!

SIBYL.   Her Highness did say "yea."

(*The door of an inner room opens, and the* QUEEN'S
     PHYSICIAN *appears.*)

PRINCESS.   Ah, Doctor — you? How fares the Queen?
     Last night

Her cheek was bridal white to match her robe.

BEN E.   The Queen is well, but anxious.   Nothing
     blights

The rose upon the cheek so soon as care.

PRINCESS.   That is most true.   Ah me, these cares of
state ! (*yawns*).
I would not wear a crown for all the world.

BEN E.   Nardi's escape is what most largely now
Contributes to the Queen's disquietude.

PRINCESS.   Nardi's escape?

BEN E.   Your Highness must have heard
How that a sudden fit of madness made
Expedient his removal.

PRINCESS.   Yes, we heard.
And so he has escaped.

BEN E.   The coach wherein,
Attended by his keepers, to a place
Of safe detention he was being conveyed,
Was, ere it had proceeded many miles,
O'ertaken by a storm among the hills,
At which the horses, it would seem, took fright,
And bolted with it down a steep incline,
Against the granite boulders at whose base
"Twas dashed to pieces.   One of Nardi's guards
Escaped with bruises and a fractured limb ;
The other, who, together with his charge,
Leapt out when first the horses ran away,
Lay stretched, when found, beside the roadway, dead.
But Nardi's self was nowhere to be seen,

Nor have we tidings gained of him as yet.
The Queen conceived your Highness might afford
Some clue that should conduct to his arrest.

PRINCESS. Who?—I ?

BEN E.   You, madam, who have deigned of late
To lavish on him favours manifold.
You, to whose presence he has been allowed
Access at will, and who have won his trust
As none before. 'Tis thought he may have held
Speech with your Highness since his late escape.

PRINCESS. Intelligencer to a lunatic
That with his keepers plays at hide and seek !
Truly the Queen and you, sir, honour me.
Perhaps she thinks I give him secret shelter
Within these walls—I do believe she does !
Will you be pleased yourself to search my rooms?

BEN E. My royal mistress harbours no such thought.
To violate your privacy I bear
No warrant, madam.

PRINCESS (*seeming somewhat mollified*). I am glad of
          that.
'Tis true that he was with us oft of late,
Diverting with his prattle and his songs
These ladies and myself. We saw him last—
When was it, Sibyl, do you recollect ?

SIBYL. I saw him, madam, in your company
On Monday last. I have not seen him since.
That I can say with truth.

VERON.   Yes, Monday 't was.

PRINCESS. You hear, sir. Of his present whereabouts
We are as ignorant as you yourself.

BEN E. One who could doubt your royal word must be
An infidel indeed ; and yet, and yet—

(*The door of the inner apartment is flung open with
violence, and the* PRINCE *appears, looking disturbed
and angry.*)

PRINCE. Cleodora, if you know the hiding-place
Of this young man, reveal it, in God's name !

PRINCESS. Why, brother, what's the matter ? You seem
moved.
Her vanished darling should the Queen deplore,
No one need wonder ; 'twere in nature, that.
But you, my Aon, might contrive, I think,
To bear his loss with equanimity.

PRINCE. Why are you always seeking to infect
My mind with jealousy ?

PRINCESS.   With jealousy ?

PRINCE. To sow before our bridal moon is old
The seeds of strife between my wife and me ?
Yes, you may smile and curl your scornful lip, —

Your scandalous suggestions I retort
Upon yourself. 'Tis not the Queen,.but you,
'Twixt whom and this young runaway have been
Enacted scenes of folly.

PRINCESS (*aside, and laughing to herself*).

              How it works !
Spite of your protestations, brother mine,
You are as jealous of the Innocent
This hour as I could wish.

      (*Enter, from within, the* QUEEN.)

           My dearest Gladys !
Why, you are pale . . . . You are not well, I fear.
You take the agitations of the time
Too much to heart.

QUEEN.   The care that carks me most
Is not imperial, but domestic. Princess,
Tell me where Nardi is.

PRINCESS.   I do not know.
How should I ? Nardi, Nardi, nothing else
But Nardi—I am weary of the name !
Why do you all three come to me ? Am I
His keeper ?

QUEEN.   If you know his place of refuge,
And hold it from his truest friends a secret,
You do him injury instead of service.

To fugitives the country is unsafe,
And I would rather sacrifice a province
Than any harm should light upon his head,
(*The* Princess *here casts a sidelong significant look at
her brother.*)
Since 'tis a good and gentle youth though wayward.
Why come to you for news of him, you ask?
Near where the heart is fixed the feet will loiter.
Thanks to the subtle teaching of your eyes,
Nardi has compassed all love's mystery.
You saw what lore his soul was set to learn,
And made the lesson easier by your help.

Princess.   I am a sort of primer, it would seem,
From which young lovers spell the rudiments.
(Ben Ephraim, *who had left the apartment, re-enters.*)

Ben E.   There is a priest, your Majesty, who craves
Speech with the Princess ; having, so he states,
Something of moment to impart.

Queen.   A priest ?
Where is he?

Ben E.   In the guardroom.

Queen.   Fetch him hither.
We'll hear this thing of moment.   It may chance
Concern the matter which we have in hand.

                         [*Exit* Ben Ephraim.

PRINCE. Cleodora, why last night did you withdraw
   Your presence from the dance ? and wherefore stood
   Your chair at supper vacant ?

PRINCESS.   I was seized
   With faintness which compelled me to retire.

VERON. 'Tis true.   I helped her Highness to her
   chamber.

PRINCE. And saw her Highness safe in bed, no doubt.
   Mendacious, both of you !   Not unobserved,
   Out in the dark you stole.   This morning marks
   Were found of footsteps near the haunted grot.
   That one or both within the last few hours
   Have verbal intercourse with Nardi held
   There is sufficient reason to believe.

   (*Re-enter the* QUEEN'S PHYSICIAN *with a* PRIEST.)

PRIEST. Which is the royal lady whom I seek,—
   Cleodora, sister of the Consort Prince ?

PRINCE. Yonder she stands, good priest. Your will
   with her ?

PRIEST (*looking towards the* QUEEN).
   Mine eyes are dazzled.   If I do not err,
   A royal presence more majestical
   Than that of even the Princess or the Prince
   Impregns this chamber.

QUEEN.   Here, as everywhere,
  A presence more majestical abides
  Than that of prince or princess whatsoe'er.
  (This priest's a courtier).   Speak your errand briefly,
  And, if its end be honest, have no fear.
PRIEST.   Unfit were I God's minister to be,
  If aught but honest, gracious Queen, it were,
  And would her Highness lend me private ear, -
PRINCE.   The Princess has no secrets from her kin.
  You can discharge yourself of anything
  That you may chance to have to say to her
  With freedom in this presence.
  (PRIEST *appears to hesitate.*   VERONICA *suddenly steps*
    forward.)
VERON.   I divine
  This good man's errand.   'T is a small affair,
  Far, far beneath her Majesty's regard.
  Might I upon the Princess's behalf,—
PRINCE.   Your mediation, kind Veronica,
  Will be invited when it is required.
                    (*To the* PRIEST.)
  Resolve your business into words at once.
PRIEST.   Then, madam, know, the youth on whom you
    meant
  Your hand this day in marriage to confer,

By soldiers of the enemy is seized,
And carried prisoner hence.

(*The* QUEEN, *who has started excitedly from her seat,
resumes it, and whispers eagerly with the* PHYSICIAN,
who stands behind her chair.)

PRINCE. What stuff is this?
The man's some mad fantastic!

VERON. Mad indeed!

BEN E. Who is the youth you speak of?

PRIEST. A young lord
Belonging to the Court, fair-haired and tall.

BEN E. The Princess meant to marry him, you said?
Explain more fully. You will best secure
Your private interest and content the Queen
By telling all you know without reserve.

PRIEST. I see no reason why I need withhold
Aught that the Queen desires me to disclose.
An honest woodman, whom I long have known,
Roused me from rest this morn while yet 't was dark,
And urgently besought me to pronounce
The nuptial blessing o'er a youthful pair
Who, two hours after daybreak, would be found
Before the altar of St. Winifred.
Suspecting something strange; for when anent
These two in such untimely haste to wed

I questioned him, he suddenly relapsed
Into his native stolidness, I gave
A qualified consent, and sought betimes
The little forest chapel which, disused
For purposes of worship, has become
A lovers' trysting-place—I seldom pass
The small dim ivied porch but I descry
Some blushing couple on the bench beneath--
From time to time a stolen peasant match,
Moreover, such as I will swear I deemed
The one in question, secretly within
Its walls the Church's sanction has received.
Arrived, I found the groom, with countenance
As young and radiant as the morn without,
(No peasant he, I saw it at a glance,)
Alone, expectant, pacing to and fro
The small flagged aisle with quick, impatient stride.
He hailed me joyfully, but ere a word
Could be exchanged between us, stealthy steps
Were heard without. The stripling, as I guess,
Deeming the bride and witnesses were come,
Rushed to the door, but quickly started back
And gave a low, sharp cry, at meeting there
Some half-a-dozen soldiers on the point
Of entering.

BEN E.   Rebel soldiers?

PRIEST.   Why, they wore
The colours of the rebel Count, and two
I recognized as men of Sars who joined
His cause, I know, not four weeks since.

BEN E.   Proceed.

PRIEST. The leader of the band advancing bade
The youth surrender.   He shook back his locks,
Folded his arms, and planted his right foot
More firmly on the ground for sole reply.
But when a hand was on his shoulder laid,
He darted forwards through their very midst,
Thrusting the men away on either side,
With such a suddenness he would have won
The open air, and possibly escaped,
But that the hindmost soldier aimed a blow
Which made him pause and stagger, when the rest
Secured him and his arms with cords confined.
And then they led him forth, with sullen scorn
He yielding since resistance nought availed,
And only turning once to cry to me,
" Acquaint the Princess "—as beneath the low
Green-mantled archway of the porch he passed.
From what I since have from that peasant gleaned,
And otherwhere, my duty, as I thought,

Couched in the young man's bidding I perceived,
" Acquaint the Princess."

BEN E.   It's a curious tale,
   Yet one that may be easily explained.
   Nardi, good youth, is weak and credulous,
   We call him here at Court " The Innocent."
   Your peasant friend, yourself, and he, 'tis clear,
   Have been the victims of some cruel hoax,
   In which the Princess all complicity
   With emphasis, be sure, will disavow.
   Nardi's unbacked assertion, I presume,
   Alone connects her Highness with the plot ?

   (PRIEST *looks confused and is silent for a moment. A
      thought then seems to strike him, and he produces from
      his pocket after some searching a crumpled piece of
      paper.*)

PRIEST.   This slip of paper was at midnight last
   From out a window of the Palace dropped
   To one who, by appointment of the youth,
   (That woodman,) to receive it stood beneath.
   I found it in the chapel, on the spot
   On which the young man with the soldiers strove.

BEN E. (*takes and reads it aloud*).
" As snow 'neath sunshine, wax in front of fire,
   I melt before the warmth of your desire ;

When morn is two hours old, steal, unespied,
And in the woodland chapel greet your bride—

" CLEODORA."

(*Hands paper to* QUEEN *and* PRINCE.)

QUEEN. Infamous !

PRINCE. I know that hand.

Lady Veronica, these lines are yours.

QUEEN. Another hand has signed them.

PRINCE. Yes, by heaven !

This shameful missive you, Cleodora, signed
And sanctioned ?

VERON. (*eagerly*). No, I wrote the whole ; I feigned—

PRINCESS (*with coolness*).

My back is strong enough to bear the brunt
Of mine own follies, good Veronica.
The signature is mine ; the rest was writ
At my dictation.

QUEEN (*to* BEN E.). We have heard enough.
Remove the priest, but let him be detained.
You and your women, Princess, to your own
Apartments will confine yourselves henceforth
During our sovereign pleasure.

PRINCESS. We shall yield
Compliance with your Majesty's desire.

QUEEN. We mean that you shall have no choice but
yield.

PRINCESS.   Am I to deem myself a prisoner, then?
Aon, do you intend to suffer this?

PRINCE.   For my sake let her not endure this shame,
Whatever for her reckless levity
She merits.   To be shut awhile in Sars
Can do your truant favourite little harm.
"Twill damp the ardour of his soaring flame,
And give his forwardness a wholesome check.

QUEEN.   Princess!   Your further presence we excuse.

PRINCESS.   This usage of your sister and your guest
May meet requital sooner than you think.

(*Sweeps superbly out of the apartment, followed by her
ladies.   The* PRINCE *stands irresolute for a few
seconds, and then goes out after them.* BEN EPHRAIM
at the same moment re-enters.)

QUEEN.   Said I not love so placed could bring but ill?
Your cunning and your prescience where were they,
When to foresee and hinder this you failed?

BEN E.   Your youth is wiser, madam, than my age.
I guessed not matters of such weight might hang
Upon a young man's fancy for a maid.

QUEEN (*after a pause, sighing*).
My brown hairs notwithstanding to your grey
Must come for counsel.   What is to be done?

BEN E.　First with your royal warrant I will search
　　Her Highness's apartments, and each scrap
　　Of writing and suspicious token seize.
　　Next I must to the camp, and thence to Sars.

QUEEN.　And based on air should your suspicions
　　　　prove,
　　How to our consort shall we justify
　　Measures so harsh and arbitrary as these?

BEN E.　It was a preconcerted thing—no chance—
　　This seizure in the chapel.　There has been
　　Collusion 'twixt the Princess, or her maids,
　　And someone yonder in the rebel host.
　　The unknown quantity which thus confounds
　　Our reckoning 't is essential we should know.

QUEEN.　At this unlooked-for juncture it were wise
　　Into our counsels to admit the Prince.

BEN E.　No, no.

QUEEN.　　　　Why not?—his Highness is a thought
　　Begrudgeful of our manifest concern
　　For Nardi, and—in short we deem it fit
　　The burthen of this secret he should share.

BEN E.　Nardi were then a mark for jealousy
　　Upon the Prince's part more perilous far.

I

QUEEN. How so? . . . Then, if this secret is to lie
    Like a drawn sword between our spouse and us,
    'Twere better far to have remained unwed.

BEN E. I wish the woman in your Majesty
    Were oftener in subjection to the Queen.

QUEEN. All natural feeling in me you would crush—
    Still every human throb. A queen of wood
    Or stone would serve your turn as well as I.
    The crown! it weighs like lead upon my brow.
    A stool of penance rather than a throne
    Is that whereon—for sins not mine—I sit.
    Oh, I did wrong to wed the man I loved!

BEN E. To give your high self unreservedly
    To bliss connubial, madam, what forbids?
    Do so, and let the kingdom's turmoil cease.
    There's one will ease you of the leaden load—
    Yield it to the Pretender, Pharamond!

QUEEN. That will I never, by my father's soul!
    Oh, why do I stand wrangling with you here
    When such important issues are at stake?
    Go, comb out this entanglement, and then—
    Commands, directions, have I none to give.
    Act as your own sagacity dictates
    For our and Nardi's safety, and the State's.

            [Exit BEN EPHRAIM. QUEEN *retires within.*

SCENE 5.—A ROOM IN THE FORTRESS OF SARS, THE
SAME AS IN ACT 2, SCENE I.
The PRETENDER *and* WITHOLD.

WIT. It 's most distinct.

PRET. Between his shoulders?

WIT. Yes.

PRET. Withold, my mother's brother's son, that sign
Emblems the difference 'twixt your blood and mine.
It is the hall-mark with which Nature stamps
Men-children of the royal race. This link
Completes of his identity the chain.
The lad seems docile?

WIT. Fairly so; keeps up
A rippling flow of converse with himself
When none is by, or weeps and wrings his hands.
But speak to him, he answers you as haught
As if already he were crowned the King.
Hark! footsteps—they are bringing him along.

(*Exit* WITHOLD.)

NARDI *enters.*

PRET. (*advancing towards him*).
I trust your slumber has been sound and sweet,
And blest with golden dreams, as youth's should be.
The needs that press upon the time must plead

I 2

Excuse for any lack of courtesy,
The violence, to wit, of yesterday,
The soldier's fare and lodging. We intend
To better your accommodation soon,
If fortune still is gracious to us. Sit.
> (*Takes his hand and draws him towards a seat,
> which* NARDI, *however, declines.*)

You know who speaks to you ?

NARDI (*surveying him carefully from head to foot*).   The
rebel Count ?

PRET.   If any tongue but yours had been so bold—
And yet the tongue that least of all has cause
To adjective my title thus is yours.

NARDI.   The Count of Ghyl was labouring to deprive
His lawful sovereign of the crown, I thought.

PRET.   The Count no lawful sovereign owns save one,—
(*Looks at him keenly and makes the slightest possible
inclination.*)

And that one does not wear the crown as yet.

NARDI.   I know but little about politics,
And care still less.   I—Nardi—am a poor
Dependent on the bounty of the Queen,
Who will not ever think it worth her while
To ransom one of such minute account.
Be generous, good my lord, and let me go.

I never wish to see the Court again.
I only want my liberty, and leave
To wander where I will.   I have some friends,
Poor friends of my own making, humble friends ;
And—and a woman cares for me and—

PRET.   Ah !
The niece or daughter of these humble friends,
Some village beauty—do I guess aright ?

NARDI (*after a moment's pause*).
She is of rank as lofty as your own.

PRET.   Would one thus lofty stoop to love a mean
Dependent ?

NARDI.   Strange though it must seem, 'tis true.
Yesterday was to be our wedding-day.
Your soldiers seized me in the chapel aisle,
Awaiting her arrival as I stood.
The priest was by the altar, book in hand.

PRET.   Forget her.   Marriage is for men, not boys.
Few wed the object of their first desire.
'T is not because we chance to fall in love,
That we must forthwith marry.   I had loved
Before my years had numbered even the few
That yours do now, and am not married yet.

NARDI.   Forget !—you never loved.

PRET.   Ah, thus eighteen
   Looks down on eight-and-thirty.   Very sad,
   To leave the summits rosy with the dawn,
   And on the plain of middle life descend
   Mid disenchanting daylight.
NARDI.   What she felt,
   When coming to the church she found me not,
   It tortures me to think!
PRET.   Oh, be consoled.
   She did not come, and did not mean to come.
   She only played with you—nay, be not vexed,
   Her charms have turned maturer heads than yours.
   She was not meant for you nor you for her.
   Proceed we now to weightier topics.   Sit,—
   For some few moments I may yet command——
NARDI.   I do not choose to sit.   It is a lie!
   You are a devil who would tempt me thus
   To doubt her love and faith!   She sent me word,
   Signed by her hand and with her seal impressed——
PRET.   That missive's only object was to place
   Your person in *my* power, for reasons high
   Which—will you but be patient—you shall hear.
   When two nights since the Princess you waylaid,
   It was to meet with me that she had thus
   Into the starless night crept forth by stealth.

Our trysting-place was nigh—the haunted grot.
There, ambushed as I stood, I overheard
Your wild appeal, and saw at once the means
Whereby a project might be realized,
Of which my mind was full.   This project was——

NARDI.   *You* are her lover then ?

PRET.   I will not hide
The fact that I do one day hope to call
The fair Cleodora " wife."   Yourself will grace
With an auspicious presence, so I trust,
Our nuptials, and will smile as through your mind
The memory of this hour's vexation flits.
Now yield me close and undivided heed,
For I have that to tell will wholly change
The aspect of your life.

NARDI.   The Princess, then,
Betrayed me ?

PRET.   Give it not so harsh a name.
The Princess lent herself to my design——

WIT. (*re-entering*) From General Morios—a despatch
which claims
Instant attention from your Highness.

PRET.   Ah ! . . . (*glances over it*).
Where is the messenger ?

Wit.   He waits without.

Pret.   Admit him.

(*Looks at* Nardi, *who has sunk into a chair with his
    elbows resting on the table and his face buried in his
    hands.*)

                         Stay—not here.   I'll come outside.

                                          [*Exeunt.*

Nardi (*alone*).

I seem as if I had been crushed and stunned
By falling headlong off some giddy height,
And slowly were awaking to a sense
Of mortal injury and pain.   Do hearts
Feel thus when broken ?   .   .   .

                         Not for boys, he said.

At what age does the heart, I wonder, reach
Maturity ? and when do we become
Worthy that women should keep faith with us ? . . .
Do people linger long with broken hearts ?
If I could die at once !—and wherefore not ?
We kill a dog to put it out of pain.   .   .   .

        (*Draws the* Princess's *dagger from his bosom.*)

Here is the coveted weapon she bestowed
That first time that I sang to her.   The point
Is sharp.   My heart, however, cannot bleed
More than it does already, thanks to her.

Did she foresee and give it me for this? . . .
Kind blade, one kiss is for the fair white hand
From whence I had you—one is for yourself,
That in a trice will cure my grief. . . .
      (*Uncovers his breast*) Now quick,
Quick to your goal!
      The PRETENDER *re-enters.*
PRET.   What's this?—Hi! Withold! here!
The boy has fainted. See to him.
WIT.   Here's blood.
PRET. My God, he has stabbed himself! . . .

ACT IV.

SCENE.—A ROOM IN THE PALACE.

The QUEEN *and* SIBYL, *the latter in tears.*

QUEEN.   I have a man's dislike to witness tears.
  Weeping will not reverse your mistress' flight.
  With you light-hearted ladies it is all
  Sunshine or floods, like tropic-island weather.
SIBYL.   My head is light more often than my heart,
  God knows !
QUEEN.   Our royal Consort, you are sure,
  Of this engagement cognizance had none ?
SIBYL.   Oh none, I swear !
QUEEN.   You need not swear.   How long
  Have Pharamond and the Princess been engaged ?
SIBYL.   Four years.   That spring she travelled for her
    health—
  Now five years since—'twas then she met him first.
  He liked her for her beauty and her wealth.
  She ever loved to play with sharp-edged tools,
  Touch pitch and shew she rested undefiled,
  And so, what first attracted her to him—
  It was I think his sinister renown.
  Well, then he followed us from place to place,

Haunted us everywhere, and pressed his suit.
She held out long but yielded in the end.
A roving schemer like Prince Pharamond,
Bankrupt in purse and reputation both,
Bold as she is, her Highness did not dare
Own as her favoured suitor to her kin.
She therefore stipulated that their love
Should rest a secret till she came of age.
The day that rounded her minority
Brought these twin pieces of intelligence—
Her brother was your Majesty's betrothed ;
Her lover was in arms against your throne.
Hence has their love been hidden till this hour,
And never have they met except by stealth.

QUEEN.   Yet, less than four years since, the Count of Ghyl
Was suitor for another hand than hers.

SIBYL.   She overlooked that treachery, but will ne'er
Forgive your Majesty for being its cause.
For that she hates you in her secret heart ;
For that the spark which Nardi from her eyes'
Contagious lovelight—Nardi, whom she deemed
Your darling—caught, she kindled into flame ;
The while with jealousy, which had this youth
For object, simultaneously she sought
To infect the Prince your spouse, so lately wed.

QUEEN.   A very pretty tissue of intrigue.

The PRINCE *enters.*

PRINCE.   The circle of investment is complete.
  The batteries on the south-west ridge are ready
  To vomit forth their thunder—the last gun
  Is in position placed.   To-day we hold
  Sars in our grip.
QUEEN.   Is that the latest news?
PRINCE.   The very latest.
QUEEN.   No; there's later still.
  Aon, your sister's gone.
PRINCE.   Gone?   What?   Gone where?
QUEEN.   Spurning behind them with their horses' hoofs
  The highway dust, their faces turned towards Sars,
  She and Veronica this morn were seen.
PRINCE.   Cleodora and Veronica—towards Sars?

QUEEN.   Yes; galled at what of late transpired, despite
  Her impudent composure at the time,
  And finding her position hourly grow
  Less tenable, no sooner was she freed,
  (At whose remonstrance you may recollect,
" I am my sister's surety," someone said,)
  No sooner was she freed from that restraint,
  To which for reasons adequate 't was deemed

Expedient to subject her, than to join
Her lover the Pretender, who for years
Contracted to her secretly has been,
She fled. With him, with Pharamond himself,
When three nights since we missed her from the
    dance,
She tryst was keeping in the haunted grot,
And Nardi to his power she then betrayed.
The Lady Sibyl will relate you these
And other things in detail when her mind
Is more composed.
PRINCE (*to* SIBYL).   I live in the dark, it seems.
    Why did you not reveal these things before?
SIBYL.   'T was not my part her Highness to betray.
PRINCE.   Yet it appears that you betray her now.
SIBYL.   The truth can now no longer be concealed.
PRINCE.   Why did you not our sister's flight partake?
SIBYL.   Her Highness having honoured me of late
    With but a maimed and partial confidence,
    I knew not that she meditated flight.
PRINCE.   Have you and she, then, quarrelled?
SIBYL.   Yes and no.
    'Twas brokerage of a cruel kind, I thought,
    And dangerous, Nardi to his rival thus
    To give in pawn—the favourite of the Queen

To the Queen's foe, and clothed my thought in speech;
The breath too bold on which my words were borne
Her friendship for me into coolness fanned,
And blew me out of favour.

PRINCE.   You shall wind
    More of this tangled skein for me anon ;
    At present with the Queen I must confer.

                                        (*Exit* SIBYL.)

PRINCE.   What shall we do ?

QUEEN (*who has been pacing the chamber in deep thought,
      with sudden vivacity*).   To rescue Nardi ?

PRINCE (*with a gesture of impatience*).   No,
    Cleodora to recall.

QUEEN.   To counteract
    The mischief she achieved before she went
    Is all my travail, not to woo her back.
    Nardi's abduction—   (*Page enters with a letter.*)
                            Sars ! Ben Ephraim's hand !
                        (*Tears it open and glances over it.*)
    You read—the writing swims before my eyes.

PRINCE (*reading*).   "Nardi, on being made to understand
    The treachery of the Princess, stabbed himself.
    He lives, and, such the nature of his hurt,
    May live some days, but hope beyond is none.
    The Count, convinced the wound was one past cure,

Surrendered him to your poor servant's charge.
Thus much am I permitted to disclose."
How? are you ill?

QUEEN.   A little faint—that's all. . . .

PRINCE.   I claim a husband's jealous right to know
What tie exists between this youth and you,
That thus affected at his fate you seem?

QUEEN.   A jealous husband's right I think you mean.
But your demand is just and natural both.
I always said you ought to have been told.
(*After a pause*) A hard and bitter lot for one so young
And gentle and ingenuous! He that paled
At sight of blood, and when an insect's wing
By accident he tore cried out with pain,
To lift a desperate hand against himself! . . .
Forgive me, friend, if I, that seldom weep,
Do weep a little now—when nature wrings me. . . .
Your sister has bereft me of a brother.

PRINCE.   A brother! You amaze me!

QUEEN.   Do I so?
'Twere more amazing had he been a lover.

PRINCE.   I am rebuked. . . . Much pain had I been
     saved.
If earlier of this consanguineal bond
I had been made aware.

QUEEN.   If you but knew
How often in your ear these last few days
I longed to pour the truth ! and thus our love,
Made turbid by suspicion, to its own
Crystalline purity at once restore ;
And into pity and forbearance change
Your nascent enmity towards Nardi, wronged
Too much already !—

PRINCE.   Wronged?

QUEEN.   Of birthright robbed,
And name, a victim and a scapegoat—*wronged !*—
Does not his kingly ermine clothe my limbs,
His crown my temples gird ?   The holy oil
Anointed an usurper.

PRINCE.   Is this true ?
I thought that when you said he was your brother,
You meant by nature not by law.   A day
Of strange discoveries is this for me !
How did it come to pass that he was thus
Excluded from hereditary right ?

QUEEN.   The tale is somewhat tragical and long.
Know that three stalwart sons my grandsire left.
The first, although a king, was crossed in love,
And ne'er would wed.   The third, while yet a youth,
Espoused a lady noble but not royal,

One only son who gave him—Pharamond.
The second, marrying later on in life,
Parent (of me) and widower both became
Within the year. The Duke my father's ways
Were such that he was always deep in debt.
At length he grew so hopelessly involved,
It seemed the only lever that could lift
And extricate him was a wealthy wife.
The Princess Alba had the richest dower
Of any royal maiden of her time.
And though his years outnumbered hers twice o'er,
And though he wooed for pelf, her guardians looked
With favour on his suit, for he was heir
Presumptive to a throne and had no son.
Not so the orphan Princess, she, whose heart
Already on another was bestowed,
With horror the projected union viewed ;
But yet, by importunities and threats
Worn out at last, she yielded in despair,
And bade them give her hand to whom they would.
PRINCE.   Poor maid !
QUEEN.   The nuptial rite was solemnized
With gay and splendid pomp, and on these shores
The pair a little later disembarked.
The old monastic palace of St. Just

K

Received them, for the fairy gardens famed
Which laugh around its sombre, frowning walls.
My father was at variance with the King,
Hence the new Duchess was not seen at Court ;
Nor much nor often was she seen elsewhere ;—
Her aspect wore the trace of frequent tears ;
In close seclusion, at her own demand,
She lived and nursed her sorrow and discontent.
The Duchess's demeanour towards her spouse
Was sullen and disdainful from the first.
Small pains took she to conquer or to hide
Her deep repugnance ; if he ever made
An effort to conciliate her regard
I know not,—the unhappy one was young,
And youth excites compassion ; she was fair—
And beauty is a challenge unto love.
This, the sole portrait of her that exists,
I found but few days since :—see Nardi's face,
With just a riper and more sensuous look ;
Nardi's gold locks in unimpeded growth,
Which reached, all natural wave and curl, her knees.
PRINCE (*examining the miniature*).

    A lovely woman—none may that deny.
QUEEN.   And yet in him she never woke the least
    Emotion, it would seem, of tenderness.

But, notwithstanding, being a man, he chafed
To find himself the object of such scorn.
Gloom on his brow, resentment in his heart,
He stalked about the place from day to day.
At length, in weariness and high disgust,
Pleading affairs, he bade a cold adieu,
Betook him to the capital, and there
His ante-nuptial habits soon resumed.
He had not long been gone when something caused
The spirits of the Duchess to revive ;
Her hitherto so mournful mien grew blithe.
Instead of pining within doors all day,
She rode, walked, drove, explored the country round,
Paid visits to the village sick and poor,
And long and lonesome woodland rambles made,
A favourite lady, one who with her came
Across the ocean from her native land,
Alone attending her ; and these, it seemed,
She grew to take delight in most of all.
One day my father suddenly returned ;
The presence of the Duchess, unannounced,
All soiled with travel as he was, he sought,
And thereupon high words between the two,
And scornful laughter on the part of one—
The lady—rose. Henceforth her haunts were watched,

Her steps were followed, though without result.
The Duchess had a sharp and rancorous tongue ;
The Duke was slow and sparing in his speech,
And when he writhed the most could least retort ;
Hence, as she barbed her shafts and winged them
    home,
Blanched, quivering lips and looks of deadly hate
Were wont how sore they rankled to betray—
And these alone, till once she so beyond
Endurance stung him with envenomed words,
An impulse of ungovernable rage
Moved him to lift the riding-whip he held
And smite her heavily across the mouth.
Many and flagrant were my father's faults,
But coarse brutality was hardly one ;
And when the Duchess from her swoon revived,
Heartfelt remorse he hastened to express.
She heard him silently, and, as he ceased,
Rose pale, and, lifting slow her bare white arm,
That flashed with gems, towards heaven, invoked
    God's curse
On him and on his child.
PRINCE.   How horrible !
QUEEN.   Neither to other ever spoke again
    During the months that intervened before

Their union's tragic ending. In due course
The Duchess was delivered of a son ;
And six weeks later, spurning babe and home,
Fled to the one she loved. The Duke pursued ;
But what occurred was never fully known.
A curtained litter in his train was borne
When he returned, from which was lifted forth
The truant consort, who the well-known walls
And faces greeted with a haggard stare.
Blood on the sleeve and bosom of her gown,
Blood on her long, bright hair, her women found—
Blood unaccounted for by any wound.
No word or sigh or moan escaped her lips,
No light of recognition ever dawned
For even a single moment in her looks ;
Strong shudderings shook her frame from time to
    time,
And then she spread her hands before her eyes,
As if to shield them from some dreadful sight ;
Poor wild, scared eyes, whose lids the angel sleep
Seemed impotent to close, whose dry, hot light
The kindly tears came never to bedew !
At last one morn my father woke to learn
That he was widowed for the second time.

PRINCE. Poor soul ! A tragic story. And the babe ?

QUEEN. Whose advent through the perilous gates of
    birth
  No laureate's hymn, no parent's welcome hailed—
  The babe, a puny, feeble creature, lived,
  But would not thrive, and cried incessantly.
  At length it made a start, grew fat and strong,
  But still continued backward for its age,
  Tardy upon its feet and with its tongue.
  And ever as it grew in size and strength
  It grew in frowardness. Strange frenzy-fits
  Seized it from time to time, and then it dealt
  Ruin on everything within its reach,
  And fought and strove with whosoever tried
  To hold it or restrain, and in the end
  Would dash itself with fury on the ground,
  And lie there, livid, foaming, and convulsed.
  At ordinary times the child was dull,
  Peevish, or sullen. It would shrink and cower
  And tremble if it met its father's eye,
  Moved by congenital antipathy.
  The parent viewed it with dislike and fear.
PRINCE. You were your father's favourite, I have heard.
QUEEN. On me, whose features like his own preserved
  The ancestral type on many a coin displayed,
  The offspring of his earlier union—me—

His love was lavished. I remember yet
How he would sit and draw me to his knee,
Smooth from my brow the swart, low-growing hair,
And sigh to think that I was not a boy.
When I was ten years old, or thereabout,
My father with the King grew reconciled,
And then we used to stay at Court, and soon
The King grew fond and made a pet of me.
Once, on the terrace yonder, as I walked,
I saw together sauntering, not remote,
Among the trees my father and the King ;
And, breaking from my governess, I ran
And joined them. Uncle caught me by the hand,
And smiled, and speaking to his brother said,
" If God were pleased to take your sickly son,
This maid of ours would make a winsome queen
Hereafter, you and I being gone to rest."
" *Queen !* " said my father, "you forget the law—
No female mounts our throne," and sudden gloom
Gathered upon his brow. " And is the law
Immutable ? It alters with the changed
Requirements of the times," rejoined the King.
" In case of such an issue, we would get
The sanction of the council of the realm
To set aside that antique feudal rule

Which bars a woman from succession—rule
In which all marrow of meaning now is dry,
And rivet the reversion of the crown
On this fresh brow."   (My father's swarthy face
Glowed a dark red.)   " Our nephew Pharamond,
Who next your Dorion now in heirship stands,
Is only royal on his father's side,
Whereas the unadulterate blood of kings
Flows in the veins of little Gladys here."
Next day the Duke went home, and, since with me
The King refused to part, he went alone.
Ere many weeks elapsed there reached us news
That Dorion, my young stepbrother, was sick ;
Later the tidings came that he was dead.
A few months after this my father's horse
Stumbled one day and threw him.   As he lay
Conscious but speechless on his bed of death,
He pointed at me feebly with his hand,
And turned his fading eyes upon the King,
Who spoke some words I did not understand,
And kissed me on the brow.   Erelong was moved
The abrogation of the ancient law,
Which (Pharamond's partisans as yet were few)
With little serious opposition met ;
And I became the heiress to the throne,

The which I mounted at the King's decease,
Mid universal popular acclaim.

PRINCE. Yet Dorion all this while was still alive?

QUEEN. Not dead, but only severed from its stock,
The royal branch struck root in alien soil.
Within a hamlet by the sea remote
The little Dorion, rightful sovereign lord
Of this wide kingdom, dwelt. The minster vault
That holds our house's immemorial dust
Contains a child's sarcophagus, 'tis true,
Whereon emblazoned, by the fitful flare
Of taper held by monkish cicerone,
Is read his name and legend, but the form
Enclosed is other than my father's son's.
Yet, though his death was feigned, the malady
Was not to which 'twas feigned his death was due.
Those frenzy fits, to seize him which were wont,
Increased in frequency and force, and bred
At length a raging fever of the brain.
The case was one in which no human skill
Could aught avail, the doctors told the Duke.
To him, who yearned for nothing half so much
As quit to be of his obnoxious heir,
This hopelessness meant hope. Each day he longed
To learn that that faint, flickering, vital flame,

Lit from his own, was out.   But lo ! one eve
In sleep profound the little patient sank,
And, when he woke, Ben Ephraim—him you know,
The Duke's physician then as now the Queen's—
His patron sought and gravely wished him joy,
Nature was victor, and the child would live.
Then a temptation to my father came
Which oft had whispered at his ear before,
But, since the conversation with the King,
Had taken tangible shape before his eyes.
That night the Duke unbosomed to the Jew.
Long hours, close-closeted, the two conferred,
And ere the Jew came forth his subtle brain
A scheme for compassing the Duke's desire
Had planned.

PRINCE.   Ah, now at length I comprehend.

QUEEN.   By strangers in a village far away
The convalescence of the child was watched.
Uneasiness or wonder in his mind
The change in his surroundings none evoked.
That fever burnt the recollection out
Of all connected with his previous state,
Leaving the tables of his memory
Characterless and clean ; and, what was best,
It also cooled and quieted his brain,

And changed his nature ;—those strange frenzy-fits
Racked and convulsed his frame no longer, health
Freshened his cheek and sparkled in his eye.
Still he was not as other children are.
He owned no laws save such as he himself
Imposed upon himself. And then, asleep
Or waking, he was always dreaming dreams
And seeing visions, which he oft mistook
For actual scenes and things, so palpable
These phantasms of imagination seemed ;
Irrational and wandering hence at times
His words appeared. Nor toys nor books loved
    he ;
And could not learn like other children, nought
Of pains availed to teach him, yet he did
By nature things that most achieve by art.
Thus, every nerve and fibre of his frame
Would thrill to music, and he played by ear
On any instrument that came to hand,
But could not learn the simplest tune by rote.
Mysterious songs about the winds and stars
And flowers he used to make, and in his clear
Child's treble sing them for his own delight
In soft recitative, which now and then
Wild sobbing gusts of melody would break.

PRINCE.   In such an union's issue one would look
   For something of abnormal and unique.
   Nature compounded him of elements
   Discordant.   How became he, under veiled
   Conditions, retransplanted to the Court?
QUEEN.   I was a three year's queen, and just seventeen,
   When by strange chance I learnt my brother lived.
   I then would gladly of the dignity
   Have stripped myself, in innocence usurped,
   But I was overruled,—and he was mad,
   They said, moreover, and unfit to reign.
   Next year I made a progress through the realm,
   And once, being nigh to where I knew he dwelt,
   I longed to see him; and Ben Ephraim, much
   Against his will and judgment, brought and placed
   The boy before me, then some twelve years old.
   My heart upleapt to meet my father's son;
   I loved him when I looked upon his face;
   And, loving him, refused to part with him.
   Ben Ephraim warned me, but I would not heed,
   For I was wilful and—I see it now,
   I see it now, when all too late—unwise.
   A member of the household thus he grew,
   And soon a household favourite—while the men
   Amused themselves with his simplicity,

The women liked him for his beauty's sake.
That is his story.   Pharamond, who learnt
The secret, how we know not, thought, no doubt,
By means of it to crutch his limping cause.
But Nardi, in his subtle innocence,
Outwits him—turns his back in high disdain
On all of us, and stretches out his arms
Boldly to God.
PRINCE.   For us and all—so best,
If you will hear me say it.   While he lived,
The crown sat never firmly on your brows.
QUEEN.   That's true.   And yet I cannot say, " so
    best."
He was a gracious creature.   Had he died
A natural death—of fever or disease,
Before my eyes—I had not grieved so much.
But oh ! to make a bloody ending thus,
By his own hand, so wantonly provoked !—
Your sister—well, we'll speak of it no more ;
We look from different standpoints . . .
                              Dearest Aon,
I'll seek my pillow and lie down awhile,
My head aches.
PRINCE.   I will bring you to your women.
                              [*Exeunt.*

ACT V.

SCENE I.—GARDENS OF THE PALACE.

Enter the QUEEN *and* SIBYL.

QUEEN. With any lady whom I so desired
To make my friend as you I never met.

SIBYL. Nor I with one I would with greater joy
Serve and companion than your Majesty.

QUEEN. If thus reciprocal our liking be,
Why to your native land will you return?
It is the Prince's wish as well as mine
That you should make this Court henceforth your
home.

SIBYL. Forbear to urge me, madam.

QUEEN. We must try
Whether our Consort's eloquence can sap
Your resolution.

SIBYL. I entreat you—no,
Let not his Highness press me—I might yield! . . .
I will confess a secret which, though some
Have guessed it, ne'er was put in words till now.
I loved—I dare not say I *love*—the Prince.

QUEEN. My husband! . . . Was the feeling mutual,
pray?

SIBYL.　Ah no! the worse—or better—hap for me.
I've nought wherewith his Highness to reproach.
From infancy Veronica and I
Were brought up with the Princess, as you know.
And, while together we were children all,
The Prince would share our pastimes.　As we grew,
His studies put divorce 'twixt him and us ;
But when he quitted college, and before
His culture was by foreign travel orbed
Into completeness, while the glowing months
Of one too brief, delightful summer flew,
We had him almost wholly to ourselves.
And—how it came to pass I scarcely know,
But he and I ere long grew friends, close friends.
No friendship 'twixt a woman and a man,
However wise and innocent, but has
A vulnerable heel for love's sly shaft,
I am sure of that—unless they are saints, or old.
He lent me books and showed me all his mind.
Together oft we strolled beside the sea
When none were witnesses except the stars,
Or when the small waves danced beneath the moon
And threw up silver foam, and converse held
Serious and sweet, and interchanged our thoughts
About all things in heaven and earth—save one.

I never thought he was in love with me.
Too gay he seemed, too unreserved, too kind.
This hope alone was mine—that I should grow
Dear to him unawares, should wind myself
Into his heart unconsciously, and he,
Finding me one day in possession there,
Be powerless to dislodge me—hope how vain!
At length to wander over distant lands
He left us.   His adieu was kind and warm,
But not a word my thirsting ear could drink
That other species of regard implied
Than brother upon sister might bestow.
When after two years' absence he returned,—

QUEEN.   Well? then?

SIBYL.   Your Majesty and he had met.

QUEEN (*after a slight pause*).

To love and not to be beloved again—
Few but endure the sharpness of that pang
Some time or other in their lives.   Poor Sibyl!

SIBYL.   Your Majesty is spared it.

QUEEN.   Why now, look —

The best medicament to cure your wound
Is marriage.   You will wed if you are wise.

SIBYL.   The wound is cicatrized.   It only aches
A little with the weather now and then.

My heart 's of other than the brittle sort,
'Twill take a mighty blow to crack it.

QUEEN.   Nay,
Hearts seldom break that much are worth. But hark,
The best thing is to marry one you love ;
The next to marry someone that loves you.
Holds the world such?

SIBYL.   I know not. Like enough.
I've had suspicions in my time. And yet .   .   .
No doubt the worst of being a woman is
One must not take the initiative in love.

QUEEN. Within three months I mate you, Lady Sibyl,
If you but give me leave.

SIBYL.   Oh, I'd trust none,
Not even your Majesty, to choose my mate.

QUEEN. Will you do better—choose your mate yourself?

SIBYL (*demurely*). Nay, madam, when I reach my native
    land
I mean to take the veil.

QUEEN.   The bridal veil,
Dear Sibyl.   [*Exeunt.*

Enter COURTIERS *and an* OFFICER.

COURT. 1.   The bombardment has begun
In earnest then.

L.

OFFICER.   We captured yesterday
The second outwork, and commence to-day
The grand assault upon the citadel.
Our batteries were already opening fire
When I left camp this morning.

COURT. 2.   Did you see
The Princess on her way to Sars?

OFFICER.   I did.
I saw her as with hair adrift and cheeks
Flushed with her headlong galop 'gainst the wind,
Sweet lips compressed, and dark eyes filled with light,
Slow through our lines she rode her smoking steed.

COURT. 1. A hare-brained lady. Did she greatly chafe
At being stopped?

OFFICER.   I think so, though she feigned
Indifference, and her young companion chid
Because she shed a perfect shower of tears
When, having vainly urged them to return,
The General said the pair must not proceed
Until the pleasure of the Queen was known
Concerning them.

COURT. 2.   Her Majesty sent word
The Princess should be suffered to fulfil
Her purpose unopposed. Is that correct?

OFFICER.   No doubt ; for when the messenger returned,
  A cavalcade of honour, to conduct
  The lovely fugitive and her damozel,
  Under protection of a flag of truce,
  Up to the gate of Sars, was straightway formed.
COURT. 1.   An episode. Well, joy attend the bride,
  Whatever one may wish the bridegroom.
OFFICER.   Bride?
COURT. 2.   Yes ; don't you know the sequel ?—then the
    Court
  Has news to tell the Camp.   'T is said that when
  The Princess and her lover met, his face
  Showed more perplexity than joy.   But love
  And policy with him go hand in hand.
  Wealth—of which Pharamond has chronic need,
  And powerful friends—which he may want ere long,
  Are hers ; and so he settled to accept
  The gift the gods had sent.   A priest was fetched,
  Who, scampering through the irrevocable words,
  Made Pharamond and Cleodora one.
  The cannon thundering from the outlying forts
  A distant trumpet-call from time to time
  Borne on the wind, the desultory fire
  Of musketry beyond the walls—such sounds
  Composed their wedding voluntary.

                              L 2

OFFICER.   How
Came you to learn all this ?
COURT. 2.   Why, you shall hear.
But let's withdraw—the Queen returns this way.

[*Exeunt.*

SCENE 2.—A ROOM IN THE PALACE.

The QUEEN *and a* MINISTER OF STATE.

MIN. (*reading from a despatch*).

" . . . . The outworks and fortifications of Sars, the
camp formerly occupied by the revolted troops, and
the citadel, lie once more at the feet of her Majesty.
. . . . Between three and six o'clock in the afternoon the admirable fire of our artillery made a breach
in the walls of the place. At six our forces were
advancing to the assault, when the garrison offered to
capitulate. I said no quarter could be granted to
rebels, and demanded unconditional surrender and
the immediate yielding up of the person of the
Pretender. This after a short delay was agreed to.
At nine o'clock our troops traversed the whole town as
well as the fortifications, while the bands played the
National Anthem. Our losses are not yet precisely
known. The troops are full of enthusiasm, and I cannot find words of sufficient praise for the courage and

coolness displayed by our young soldiers, or for the
good dispositions made by the officers."

QUEEN.   So ends this internecine strife.   Henceforth
Five letters spell the history of my reign,
And let it form an anagram of peace.

MIN.   Hither his Highness the Prince Consort comes,
Hot from the scene of action.

QUEEN.   In good time.

The PRINCE *enters.*

PRINCE.   The necks of your rebellious subjects lie
Beneath your foot, my Queen.   The siege is o'er.
I saw the breach made ; entered Sars ; beheld
The Count of Ghyl deliver up his sword,—
He did it with an air of easy grace,
Like one who less surrenders than bestows.

QUEEN.   The traitor Morios ?

PRINCE.   He is dead.   A shell,
Which during the bombardment near him burst,
So shattered both his legs the surgeon's knife
Was needed.   He the remedy endured
With philosophic fortitude ; it proved
Of small avail, however, for his death
Ensued within an hour.   He thus is spared
The traitor's fitting doom.

QUEEN.   Best so. My lord,
　　Let, at the Church of Saint Eustachius, Sars,
　　A solemn service be to-morrow held ;
　　Ourselves and royal household will attend,
　　And give to God, for strengthening our weak hands
　　To crush this insurrection, grateful praise.

MINISTER.   Your Majesty's command shall be obeyed.

                              [*Exit* MINISTER.

PRINCE.   Cleodora, hearing of my presence, begged
　　An interview, which I refused to grant.
　　It is a fact that Pharamond and she
　　Are married.

QUEEN.   Could you aught of Nardi learn ?

PRINCE.   'T was one of my first thoughts. He lingers
　　　yet.
　　I saw Ben Ephraim—" Let the Queen," he said,
　" If she would look upon his face once more,
　　Ere its soft lines grow rigid, come at once."

QUEEN.   I am for Sars then.

PRINCE.   Yes, to-morrow.

QUEEN.   No,
　　To-night.

Scene 3.—Timothy's hut as in Act III., Scene 3.
Timothy *asleep on the floor with an empty bottle in
his outstretched hand. Someone without knocks at the
door.*

Tim. (*wakes and calls out*) Morra ! . . .
Morra, I say !—get up, you lie-a-bed !
 (*Sits up and rubs his eyes. Knocking repeated.*)
Who's there ? Unbolt the door, you jade, d'ye hear ?
Curse her—where is she ? . . .
 (*Rises with difficulty. Knocking repeated more loudly.*)
(*Sings as he staggers to the door.*)
  "The bottle it is my only love,
   The bottle it is my dear——"
   . . . Shaking a man's house
About his ears. . . Come in, in the devil's name !
 (*Withdraws the bolt. Priest and some people of
 the village enter.*)
A Woman. Tim, Morra's dead !
Priest.   It 's true, your daughter 's dead.
'T would seem as if, on learning that the youth
Who so befriended her was shut in Sars,
She must as far have followed as the camp,
Where several testify to having seen
And spoken with her. Gone a week, what time

The soldiers cooked their supper, up she came,
And begged for food, and ate like one that starved.
Then, stretching towards the fort her long, lean arms,
She asked when Sars would be the Queen's again,
And if all prisoners then would be released ;
And said she had a friend within the walls.
Her eyes were wild, and, as she moved away,
Laughing a foolish laugh, they deemed her crazed.
That night much rain fell and the air was chill.
When the patrols next morning made their rounds
They found her dead behind an old stone wall,
Where, without doubt, for shelter she had crept.
Want and exposure caused her death, 't is thought—
A dreary finish.

TIM. (*straightening himself*). Friends, you see a man
  Unchilded. Friends,—(*begins to blubber*,) my only
    comfort's gone !

A MAN. Poor Tim !—a kindly man with all his faults.

A WOMAN. Lord love him ! ay, it 's nothing but the
  drink
  That spoils him.

ANOTHER MAN. Mate, cheer up !—Where go'st thou,
  Tim ?

TIM. Into the blessed air !
      (*Staggers out through the doorway.*)

ANOTHER WOMAN.   God comfort him !
What with the bad news and the drink together
He's dazed.

> [*Exeunt all, following* TIMOTHY.

SCENE 4.—NIGHT. A VAULTED CHAMBER IN THE FOR-
TRESS OF SARS, LIGHTED BY A SINGLE SUSPENDED
LAMP. NARDI *in bed and lying motionless, and* BEN
EPHRAIM.

Enter the QUEEN *and the* PRINCE.

QUEEN.   How changed !

PRINCE.   He seems unconscious.

BEN E.   No, oh no !
His mind was clear not many minutes since.
Let the Queen speak to him, her voice may rouse him.

QUEEN.   Nardi !

NARDI (*stirs and murmurs*).   The Princess will not scorn
    you, nay.
Poor little Morra ! . . . Ah, you think too much
About your plainness and deformity.
Some have straight bodies and the soul deformed,
That is the worst by far.

QUEEN.   He knows me not !

 (BEN EPHRAIM *adjusts the pillows so as to raise him*
  almost into a sitting posture, whereupon he opens
  his eyes, and his gaze wanders round the apartment
  —suddenly it is arrested, as if by some object amid
  the gloom.)

NARDI. I say I do not like that dark, stern man,—
 Send him away, he always frowns on me. . .
 Who is the woman with the long bright hair
 Bedaubed with blood, and blood upon her breast ?

QUEEN. He sees the spectral dead !

BEN E.   Nardi, you dream.
 See you not who is present ? Look—the Queen !
 You know that you were asking for the Queen.

NARDI. The Queen ?—I recollect. I think my mind
 Wanders a little. . . Madam, let me speak
 A word with you in private.

(*The* PRINCE *and* BEN EPHRAIM *at a sign from the* QUEEN
   withdraw.)

QUEEN.   They have gone.
 We are alone. What is it you would say ?

NARDI (*speaking in a weak and laboured manner at first,*
  but gaining strength and fluency as he proceeds).
 I would remind you of the hour when first,

A child, I stood before you six years back.
Your Majesty was near about the age
That I am now, I think.   You sat alone
(Do you remember ?) in a chamber small,
Whose casement opened on the stormy sea,
Then darkly flushed with sunset, while the sky
(I see it now) was filled with drifting clouds
That looked like wind-borne petals of a rose,
When Doctor Ephraim led me by the hand
Into your presence ; and you left your seat
And stood and gazed at me with lips apart,
And suddenly you came and threw your arms
About my neck and kissed me, and I heard,
Despite the surging of the sea without,
The beating of your heart.   Then something said
By Doctor Ephraim in a chiding tone
Made you draw back, but on my cheek a tear
Of which mine eyes were innocent remained.

QUEEN.   Something of this I own I recollect.

NARDI.   And in the sunlight of your favour since,
Which has not once been clouded, have I lived.
Like a strong shield your love has interposed
Between the world and me, and few have dared
To slight or scorn me with impunity.
And now and then an indescribable

Proud sense of isolation I have felt,
An impulse to command, as if I had
Kings' blood in me. And I have pondered much
From time to time, and, putting this and that
Together, guessed some secret natural bond
Unites me to your Majesty. The Duke,
Your father, was he also mine?

QUEEN (*in a low voice*).   He was.

NARDI. Who was my mother?

  (QUEEN *seems to hesitate.*) Ah! I see, I know—
Pardon!—it is not right to speak of her.

QUEEN. Your mother was our father's second wife,
 The Duchess Alba.

NARDI.   *Duchess Alba!* . . then—
  (*In a wondering awe-struck whisper.*)
Was I the little boy that died?

QUEEN.   The Duke's
Sole son, Prince Dorion, the kingdom's heir.

NARDI. But was I put aside then? Why? Because—
Ah! " the Queen's Innocent "!

QUEEN.   No, not for that,
 Not wholly, (ah, my God, what can I say?)
 Nardi, my angel, oh forgive the dead!

NARDI. Is that our father yonder?—look!—

QUEEN.   Where, where?

NARDI.   Why does he always frown ?   I *hate* him !

QUEEN.   Hush !

Oh hush ! there's no one here but you and I.

Speak not of hate !

(*He sinks back as if exhausted, and shuts his eyes.*)

NARDI (*after a pause*).   You kissed me that first day.

Will you not kiss me now ?

QUEEN (*kissing him tenderly*).

                                    My own dear brother ! . . .

Are you in any pain ?

NARDI.   No pain . . . no pain . . .

My wound is nearly well . . . I seem to sink

So low among the pillows !

(QUEEN *raises his head and supports it against her shoulder.*)

                                    One more kiss . . .

Is it not almost time to send for lights ?

(*Enter, after a few minutes, the* PRINCE *and* BEN EPHRAIM.)

QUEEN.   Ben Ephraim, is this sleep or—?

BEN E.   It is sleep

Sounder than he has slept for eighteen years.

PRINCE.   At length then you are Queen without a rival.

QUEEN (*laying* NARDI'S *head back upon the pillow*).

Seldom does parting with a rival give

So sharp a pang as I experience now.
Thus young!

BEN E.   His life, though brief, has been intense.
What could the years do more for him?   He lived
And loved and wept and sung, he tasted life—
Its bitter and its sweet—right through to the core,
Crowding enough emotions in eighteen
To furnish forth threescore.   To such as he,
Death's not untimely, though it comes betimes.

PRINCE.   Bid him a long farewell and come away.

> (*Leads her off as* BEN EPHRAIM *draws the sheet over*
> NARDI'S *face.*)

SCENE 5.—A ROOM IN THE FORTRESS.

The PRINCESS *and* VERONICA.

VERON.   As she forgives she hopes to be forgiven.
She thought we used her ill, and thinks so yet;
And, after we had fled without a word,
She owns that she denounced you to the Queen,
With whom a league of friendship she has formed.
She wished, and had prepared, to start for home
But now, at this disastrous juncture, feels
Her place is by your side.   She recollects
The joyous years we three have spent together,

And in your sorrows also claims her share.
Ah, madam, will you render incomplete
The dear harmonious triad? Do you still
Refuse to see our Sibyl?

PRINCESS.   Her allegiance
Is full of limitations and conditions.
Sibyl, instead of drifting with my mood
As you do, loves to pull against the stream.
Her will is too stiff-necked and combative.
You suit me best, and yet—I want her too.
To be without her is like leaving off
A garment one is used to. Fetch her hither.

> (*Exit* VERONICA, *who comes back, after a few seconds,*
>   *with* SIBYL.)

Ah, Sibyl, you return to me!

SIBYL.   Dear Princess,
I never left you, that you know right well.

>   (*They embrace.*)

PRINCESS. Oh, Sibyl, does the trial still proceed?

SIBYL. I am not sure if yet the Court have risen.
"Twas thought that sentence would be given to-day.

PRINCESS. I think 'tis given already, and you know
More than you have the courage to impart.

SIBYL. Your Highness should prepare your royal mind
To hear the worst. I know no more than this.

PRINCESS (*impatiently*).

Will no one cheer me with a little hope,

Even if it prove a false one in the end?

SIBYL.　That, madam, were the act of a false friend.

PRINCESS.　Against us is our brother much incensed?

SIBYL.　The Queen and he are one in all their thoughts.

PRINCESS.　Ah, when a man so doats on—what is that?

SIBYL.　Something that I must hand you from the

　　Queen.

　　(*Presents a packet.* PRINCESS *opens and drops its*

　　　　contents upon the floor.)

VERON.　Your dagger which you gave "The Inno-

　　cent" ! . . .

　　　　　　　　　　　　　　(*Picks it up.*)

They say it was with this he stabbed himself.

PRINCESS.　Is that wet blood on it?

VERON.　　　　　　　　　　No, only rust —

　　How foolish !

PRINCESS.　　　　But it may have been his blood

　　That rusted it . . . You—Sibyl—did you know

　　What ghastly token you were to deliver?

SIBYL.　No, or I would have humbly begged the Queen

　　To choose some other bearer, that I vow.

　　She said it was a trinket she desired

　　That you should re-possess.

PRINCESS (*with a shudder of disgust*).

                    A trinket—pah !

Now I shall dream of him to-night, I know,

· Dream that I see him with his breast all bare

And bleeding, as I did but two nights since.

(*Door opens, a glitter of bayonets is seen for a moment, and the* PRETENDER *enters.*)

PRET.   Cleodora, I am come to say farewell.

PRINCESS.   Farewell!—Oh heavens, the sentence then is

    death !

PRET.   No, though for your sake it were well it were,—

    For then you would be free. Yet death it was ;

    But, exercising her prerogative,

    Queen Gladys has the sentence overruled,—

    Wherefore commuted to imprisonment

    Lifelong within some fortress now it stands.

    This very evening forth I fare, though what

    May be my destination know not yet.

VERON.   And this for seeking to regain your just

    And natural rights !

PRINCESS.   Oh, why did you not fly,

    When flight I urged ?

PRET.   You urged the impossible.

    Flight ! Why I could not if I would have fled.

    It may be that I would not if I could.

                          M

It is not in the moment of defeat
That I forget the blood of which I come,
Or that I am a soldier.   When we stake
And lose, there's nothing for it but to pay.

PRINCESS.   And what of me? Must I your prison share?

PRET.   Nay, not so cruel-kind, so bitter-sweet
As that, my sentence.   Dear, without reproach,
You do not love me well enough, I think,
To care to suffer with me.

PRINCESS.   Pharamond!
Surely my constancy has stood some test!

PRET.   'T was depth, I thought of, more than constancy.
Not those who most inspire love, love the most.
Perchance the greatlier blest are those who love.
The boy who bled for you was nearer God
Than you whose beauty lit him to his death.
But still, to be the star of men's desire
Is something.

PRINCESS (*weeping*).   I do love you—yes, as much
As I to love am able.

PRET.   I believe it.
I almost wish, as things have fallen out,
We had not married.

PRINCESS.   Do not say so ! Yet—
And yet it had been best, no doubt.   What use

In being man and wife, if granite walls
Must frown between us ever?

PRET (*with a sigh*).   What, indeed! . . .
Now of your future let us talk a little.
The Queen will never pardon you your share
In Nardi's death; but with the Prince, your brother,
Sooner or later you will make your peace.

PRINCESS. My share! Now Pharamond, you are like the
  rest.
Could I foresee that he would kill himself?

PRET. No, no, of course not. . . . Listen; you will
  take
The initiative, and sue to be allowed
To go, with escort such as fits your rank,
Home to your native land and to the King
Your uncle. I must needs say something now
The saying of which dispense with I would fain.
'Twere hard a woman beautiful and young,
And rich and royal—one for love of whom
Youths dash their life-lamps out—to widowhood
Perpetual should be sealed—so mark me well.
If you can get advised of any means
Whereby our nuptial knot may be untied,
Of any legal informality

Which, urged, might make the marriage void,
employ—
Plead it without remorse or ruth for me.
Dissolve our hasty union ; slip your neck
From out this ill-adjusted yoke ; from me,
Dismasted, cut your gilded pleasure-craft
Adrift—you understand ?

SIBYL.   For this I'd rest
His widow all my days !—Ah, tell him, madam—

VERON. (*plucking her by the sleeve*).
Sibyl ! you foolish Sibyl ! hold your tongue !

PRINCESS (*weeping*).
No, I shall wed no other while you live !

PRET.   Hereafter this resolve.   One last embrace. . . .
Sibyl—Veronica—a hand of each.
Be happy, ladies.   To your love and care
The Princess I bequeath.
                        Farewell! . . . Farewell!

[*The* PRINCESS *sobs and clings to him.   He forcibly
    disengages himself and goes out.   The bayonets
    glitter for an instant, then the door closes.*

OTHER POEMS.

THE ETHEREAL PILGRIM.

Seed of the Eternal, destined to be blown
Hither and thither, till upon the right
Congenial soil it happen to alight ;
Voyager from the land of the Unknown,
Drifting now here now there, until some fit
And kindly port receive and harbour it.

GOD sent a Thought among the minds of men.
Some thoughts repair to us as birds do, when
They come and beat against the window-pane
Their wings a moment and are gone again ;
Or like the vision of a ghostly face,
Which has evanished into empty space
Ere one can seize its traits : but there are some
That willingly would make our minds their home,
That stand upon the thresholds of the same
And seem our hospitality to claim ;
But whom too oft, instead of welcoming,
With cold contempt away from us we fling,
Or while they stand, mute suppliants, let some mean
Familiar fancy thrust itself between
And take possession of our whole regard.
Yet, if they come across us afterward,

By holiest art with patient hand portrayed
In painting's hues, or marble ; or arrayed
In harmonies sublime, or in the glory
Of deathless numbers, or in oratory ;
Embodied in some high utility—
Discovery or invention it may be—
Which makes the springs of life more smoothly act :
Or realized in some great historic fact ;—
If those same thoughts which came to us of yore
Naked from God, should visit us once more
Thus clothed, they meet with no such rude rebuff,
We entertain them courteously enough.

* * * * *

God sent among men's minds a pilgrim Thought.
It came athwart a merchant first, who sought
His counting-house with many a hurried stride,
Whose brow was knit, and who was haggard-eyed,
Along the city's teeming thoroughfares.
A multitude of hungry clamorous cares
The audience-chamber of his mind invaded ;
Amid the sordid throng to thread its way did
That meek immortal strive, though shrinking ever
From soil of such base contact—vain endeavour !
Jostled and buffeted and overborne,
'T was forced erelong, with tarnished wings and torn,

Back through the portal, out into that same
Dim fathomless Inane from whence it came.

     *   *   *   *   *

One who had ceased to deem herself a child,
Though, by her infantile sweet looks beguil'd,
It seemed to others that she scarcely stood
Upon the threshold yet of womanhood,
Adown a road 'twixt English hedgerows stroll'd,
Before the lustrous morn was three hours old ;
Humming the air of some familiar song,
And gathering wild-flowers as she went along.
Monk's-hood, and swallow-wort, the speedwell blue,
And honeysuckle from which she shook the dew,
Vagrant convolvuli that, trailing down,
O'erfell her fresh and dainty morning gown,
The wild-briar rose and the forget-me-not,
With bracken and the hart's-tongue, she had got
Almost as many as her hand could hold.
Her hat hung on her arm, the breeze made bold
To lift the tendrils of her silk-soft hair.
O'erhead the dazzling heavens were everywhere
Without a cloud, a morn divine it was ;
The foot-worn patch of common road-side grass,
Dew-drenched, and with the early sunlight on it—
No costliest jewel-work could have outshone it.

Sudden a skylark from his nest, low hid
The other side the hedge the corn amid,
Uprose, the girl stood still and watched him soaring
Into the blue, his joyous soul outpouring ;
Our pilgrim seized the moment fortunate,
Embarked upon that stream of song, and straight
Was carried through her ears into her mind ;—
A beautiful sweet-smelling place, a kind
Of bower, with wilding fancies clambering
And running riot over everything ;
Where late—its petals only half dispread,
Although its subtle scent impregnated
Even her remotest musings—had upsprung,
That bloomy tangled overgrowth among,
A crimson flower, yshapèd like a star,
" Love" it is called in our vernacular.
Upon the uninvited guest she bent
A look of gentle, wistful wonderment,
This girl, and fell forthwith into a fit
Of mild abstraction contemplating it,
So that the sound of footsteps drawing near
Behind her struck unheeded on her ear,
And when a voice pronounced her name close by,
She gave a start and turned confusedly.
That flower's own tell-tale hue flamed up and spread

O'er cheek and throat and brow its lovely red ;
The pilgrim Thought was banished from her ken,
And flitted forth into the void again.

      *   *   *   *   *

    It came across a far-descended prince,
A man of taste and culture, prone to evince
When any lovely thing soe'er, revealed
By earth or heaven, to his regard appealed,
Delighted recognitions.   Italy
His country was, and none more prized than he
The arts called fine ; the sculptor's, so it seemed,
And poet's being those he most esteemed.
Himself a studio had—whence many a chaste
Y-carven bust that in his palace graced
Staircase or library or corridor ;
Himself a sonnet could indite of more
Than mediocre merit, did he choose,
As sometimes chanced, to trifle with the muse.
His highness sought one day the sculpture room,
To view the latest work, of one to whom
Art had, through many a dedicated year,
No pliant mistress proved, but an austere
Divinity, whose favour at the price
Was bought of vigil, fast, and sacrifice ;
Although he in her service won the crown

At last and guerdon of a great renown.
Few could unmoved that sculptured piece regard ;
The passionate story of the pair ill-starr'd,
Whose love burned clear and steadfast mid the hell
It gained for them, as that unquenchable,
Of Paolo and Francesca—handled much
By art, yet aye unworn beneath its touch,
Like love itself—the subject had suggested.
Upon the folio, on their knees which rested,
He held her right hand prisoned close in his,
And clasped her waist with his left arm, that kiss
So fatal-exquisite, of all their woe
The harbinger, while bending to bestow.
Passive accomplice in the sweet transgression,
Her gentle features wore a mixed expression,
In which confusion, rapture, tears partook ;
New-kindled passion trembled in his look.
The whole was admirably executed.
The princely dilettante, a reputed
Critic, began to cross his arms and knit
His brows, in silence contemplating it,
When what appeared an unconnected thought
Struck him, and hold of his attention caught
Distractingly. . . . The sculptor, with an eye
Of still enthusiasm, though modestly,

Viewing the product of his hand and brain,
Who stood not far removed, began to explain
Some detail ; gently starting, as he spoke,
His Highness from his reverie awoke,
And simultaneously dismissed, with scant
Politeness, that celestial visitant.

*   *   *   *   *

There was a University Professor,
A man of vast attainments, the possessor
Of an enormous stock of erudition.
Indisputably held the first position
Among the scholars of his period, he.
A man of inconceivable industry,
Moreover.   He had edited Catullus,
Lucretius, Horace, Virgil, and Tibullus,
And Homer, all with copious annotations ;
And published half a cartload of translations,
Pamphlets, lay sermons, essays critical,
Reviews of books—the catalogue of all
His labours is too long for me to quote.
The learned languages he spoke and wrote
More purely than his mother tongue, men said ;
And he could, like De Quincey, as he read
The morning journal turn it into Greek.
One eve this mighty Don stepped forth to seek

Repose and recreation for his powers,
High-tasked, at dew-fall mid his garden flowers.
Flowers were, I think, the sole things other than
His books he loved ; a childless, spouseless man,
He lavished all his wealth of tenderness,
No vast amount, yet many a one has less,
On these. Their gradual development
It yielded him an exquisite content
To watch from day to day. He did not care
To deck his rooms with them,—he could not bear
To see them plucked—but used to like to stand,
Fondling them at the same time with his hand,
And drink their breath as o'er them lover-wise
He leaned, and on their colours feast his eyes,
While on their stems they grew. And when they died,
Or by the storm were scattered far and wide,
Or fell to pieces overblown, with pains
Religious he collected their remains,
And sepulchred them in a vase antique
O'erwrought with lovely fancies of the Greek.
This evening as the pathway up and down
He paced, his hands behind him 'neath his gown,
And on some lines of Virgil meditated,
That fugitive divine, who only waited
A kindly moment—that empyreal one—

Stood suddenly before him; whereupon
He viewed it for some seconds with a hard,
A cold, inquisitorial regard;
Dragged it towards the light and turned it round,
Surveyed it from all points, and when he found
That nothing of it he could make, for under
Such harsh, unfriendly usage (and no wonder!)
All pale and wan and lustreless it grew,
And shrank and trembled as a flame will do
In an unsympathetic atmosphere,
He bade it vanish in a tone severe.

    *   *   *   *   *

Along a mighty stream whose banks rose sheer,
Their tropic garniture the water clear
Sweeping, the trees which overhung their heights
Festooned with scarlet-flowered parasites,
Forms of heroic mould and dusky hue,
Grass-cinctured, each propelling a canoe
Laden with spoils and weapons of the chase—
Some seven—did with the racing current race.
Upon a hunting expedition in
The interior of the island they had been,
And now to reach their tribal station, neighbouring
Upon the coast, ere fall of night were labouring.
The river by-and-by described its last

Curve, and behold! the estuary, which fast
They were approaching, and, beyond, that ocean
(The low, hoarse, rhythmic murmur of whose motion
Might now be heard) which we " Pacific " call,
Far stretching to the western heavens, then all
Ablaze with sunset.   The canoes shot on
With unabated speed excepting one,
The seventh, which lagged, and in another minute
Moved with the stream alone.   The savage in it
Had ceased to paddle, and was leaning slightly
Forwards with outstretched chin, his elbows lightly
Resting upon his thighs, his gaze intent
On that sky-spectacle magnificent ;
Aiming weak shafts of childish speculation,
The while with open-mouthèd expectation,
The sun its ocean-reflex he did wait
To see first kiss and then annihilate.
A sunset fiercely beautiful !—the air
Dry-clear—no intimation anywhere
Of aught to interrupt or to absorb
The intense, far-spreading radiance.   But the orb
Majestic borders on the horizon's rim,
Another moment and its lower limb
Will touch, and see ! it does, and more than touch ;
And now above the same a segment much

Diminished—now the smallest possible arc
Of its circumference—now the merest spark
Or point of living light remains alone ;
You hold your breath an instant—it is gone !
The hollow cloudless hemisphere is left
Suddenly vacant, desolate, bereft ;
And night is stealing swiftly on her way
To shroud the lifeless relics of the day.
His deep-set eyes the Uncivilized had got
Riveted motionlessly on the spot
From whence he watched that last spark disappear,
And, as he still kept gazing, one large tear
Down either cheek of dusky grain did roll.
All avenues and inlets to his soul
At this high moment were unsentinell'd—
That heavenly vagrant entered, and beheld
A dim-lit region peopled by a few
Barbaric virtues ; vices one or two
Which had not learnt to put on virtue's dress,
But in their own rude native nakedness
Exposed themselves without reproach or shame,
And superstitions—children of that same
Impenetrable mystery which surrounds,
Baffles, bewilders, awes, disturbs, confounds
Our wisest—common to his tribe and race,

N

Dwelt also in that primitive strange place.
Erelong a little gentle tremor shook
The wild man's frame, and straightway he betook
Himself to paddling his canoe once more.
Within a beached cove he leapt ashore
At length, and dragged his bark from out the tide,
The other six, drawn high and dry, 'longside,
And of its spoils to empty it was stooping,
When savage figures like himself came trooping
Out from behind the rocks and towards him ran,
And formed a group about him, and began
To enter into voluble narration,
With wild grimacing and gesticulation
Accompanied.   'Twould seem at dawn that day
A ship with sails had anchored in the bay,
And nearly half the tribe, thereof informed,
Went out and in canoes around it swarmed.
A certain number were allowed to climb
The vessel's side, and wander for a time
Freely about the deck, but by-and-by
The pale-faced men enticed them treach'rously
By twos and threes below, where, being arrived,
By those white demons they were gagged and gyved
And thrust with blows and oaths into the hold.
('This was the substance of the tale they told

To him who, with his hunting-spear in hand,
Motionless as some statued bronze did stand.)
When, two excepted—from their captors they
By dint of fierce resistance broke away,
And swam to shore though wounded—all were made
Secure and safely stowed, the vessel weighed
Anchor and straightway flew the gale before.
One of those speakers violently tore
A bandage off of healing leaves and showed
A cutlass wound from which the blood still flowed ;
Another who had climbed—his two young sons
Chancing to be among the outraged ones—
The vessel's side and to the bulwarks clung,
And when she started on her way still hung
Thereto, nor till they maimed him would desist,
Held up his hand nigh severed from the wrist.
Our hero of the sunset, as he heard
The story, hardly interposed a word,
But a wild sense of wrong, a passionate
Fierce thirst for vengeance, an immortal hate,
Seized him, and swept out every milder kind
Of thought which had been lingering in his mind.

   * * * * *

  There was a poet, on his cloak outspread
Who lay, his bent arm pillowing his head,

        N 2

Mid the cool twilight of a forest nook,
One sultry August afternoon. A book,
Open face downwards, did his breast encumber,
For he was reading when a gentle slumber
Stole in upon his senses unawares.
A young man quite he seemed, although grey hairs
In plenty mid his brown you could descry,
And though a tired worn look, which might imply
That he was one who had been introduced
Betimes to care, or else that he was used
To suffering of some kind, was on his face.
While thus, in this most choice, secluded place,
Far from the city's din, full length among
Green lights and glooms and overshadowings flung,
He lay, that houseless child of God did wend her
Towards his mind, and flashed a sudden splendour
The tranquil twilight of his dream athwart.
A playful breeze did all at once upstart,
And cause among the leaves a stir and bustle,
Then, sweeping o'er the grass with gentle rustle,
Deliciously upon his temples blew ;
Whereat the slumberer's eyelashes upflew.
Soon, on his hand uplifting half his weight,
Upon the shifting shapes with which his late
Siesta teemed, that hardly yet were faded,

He fell a-musing ; something which evaded
His memory's grasp there seemed—he racked his
  brain—
And presently it broke on him again.
Though but a naked thought, and not attended
This time by aught of luminous or splendid,
He recognized *the immortal* in its looks,
Just (so we read in the old story books)
As in the beggar-maiden at a glance
Cophetua knew his queen-to-be.   Oh chance !—
He hailed, he welcomed it, he seized, he stayed it ;
Without a moment of delay he made it
Eternally his own, and in the heat
Of inspiration leaping to his feet,
(For what is it to be inspired but thus
To know great thoughts when they do come to us
And boldly grasp them ?) he began to pace
Backwards and forwards with a flushen face,
And quick'ning pulse, and eager lips and parted,
And eyes that through their moisture lightnings darted.
And like a seed that lies within the earth ;
Or like an infant previous to its birth ;
Or like a beauteous lady jealously
Guarded from every save her lover's eye
In some rich lonely mansion ; or inspired

Fanatic of the orient, world-retired
Within a desert-mountain cave, from whence
Issue he will to kindle an intense
Enthusiasm some time among mankind—
That thought henceforth abode within his mind.
Amid the day's distractions never quite
Forgot, and mingling with his dreams at night.
Changes from time to time it underwent,
And slow mysterious development.
And if he looked on any lovely sight,
Sunset or work of art, or felt the might
Of a fair face, or moving music heard,
This thing with which his brain was quick appear'd
To throb within it.   Yearnings vague would rise,
And silent spasms convulse him, and his eyes
By reason of uncalled-for tears grow blind,
At other times when mingling with mankind.
The pleasure never palled upon his soul
Of its society, which oft he stole
To solitary places to enjoy,
And hours on hours would spend without employ
Save that of contemplating it,—content.
A lover, he, who as the seasons went,
Instead of wearying with possession grew
Enamoured more and more, till nought would do

But he and this beloved one must unite
Before the world.   He set it in the light
Of his imagination, which invested
With charm resistless all whereon it rested.
To deck the naked body of the thought
That subtle artificer, his fancy, wrought
Moreover many a sparkling ornament.
And after months—nay, after years—were spent,
He clothed it in a nuptial garb of verse ;
And thus arrayed, for better or for worse,
Tricked like a bride with gem and flower, he lent it
His name, and forth into the wide world sent it.
           *   *   *   *   *
    Some lyric stanzas from it by a young
Composer set to music were, and sung
In almost every land from north to south ;
The merchant heard them from his daughter's mouth :
The little morning saunterer, now a wife,
Sang them to that beloved one whose life
Was interwoven for evermore with hers.
With other volumes from the publisher's
The poem to the scholar went one day ;
Beside his desk with leaves uncut it lay
Whole weeks, for he professed to entertain
For modern poesy a high disdain ;

One night though, being in a listless fit,
The book he opened and dipped into it,
Thinking to read perhaps a page or two,
But ere he laid it down he read it through
To the last line, and from his pompous pen
Appeared a lengthy notice of it when
Next month the quarterly reviews came out.
The savage of the great South Sea—I doubt
If that Immortal visited his brain
Ever, in any shape or guise, again.
But when a few years later, worn and weak,
With an autumnal hectic on his cheek,
A glazed and fitful brilliance in his eyes,
To wile the winter 'neath more genial skies,
To Italy in fact, to which his fame
Had travelled long before, the poet came ;
No one evinced towards the invalid
Such kindness, none so welcomed him as did
That dilettante prince.   And as they sat
And talked one day, these two, grown friends, of that
Which was the joy of both and life-vocation
Of one, the prince, to give an illustration
And proof of something he had lately said,
Smilingly took a volume down and read
With faultless English accent, and a voice

The most melodious ever heard, and choice
Appropriate gesture certain passages,
The ones he most delighted in, from—yes,
That work—the structured outgrowth and the flower
Of that sweet living germ which in an hour·
Forgotten was rejected by the blind
And unreceptive soil of his own mind.

BALLAD OF THE MOON.

I.

I am the lady of the sky,
The maiden moon so pure and cold ;
    The same of whom in days gone by
Such tales the idle poets told ;
    Tales which had not one word of truth ;
A friend to lovers from of old,
    I needs must love, myself, forsooth !

2.

Oh, things more wild and strange are done,
More thrilling far, within my view,
    Than e'er take place beneath the sun ;
One half what I am witness to
    'Twixt dusk and dawn, in one brief night,
If any poet only knew,
    What moving poems he might write !

3.

I cross that range of mountains men
Have christened after me ; down deep
    Ravine and into savage glen
Take many a sly and slanting peep ;
    And into caverns fling my light
To glisten, quiver, shoot, and leap
    Like white flame mid the stalactite.

4.

Of many another mountain chain
I make the snowy scalps more white ;
   I steal, where some lone Memphian fane
Lies open to the ambrosial night,
   Along the hushed sphinx-guarded aisle ;
I laugh, down-gazing from my height,
   Where foam the cataracts of the Nile.

5.

I linger tenderly on shores
Of lovely warm East Indian isles ;—
   The fierce white surf for ever roars
And thunders, and the crocodiles
   Come down from the lagunes inland
To bask, and cocoa-palms for miles
   Lattice my light upon the sand.

6.

My face, which makes the stars burn dim,
In many a watery glass I view ;
   O'er one—so fair ! its crater-rim
All clothed with tree-fern and bamboo —
   I hung last night in ravishment ;
A sweet, still lake of deepest blue
   Filling an old volcano-vent.

7.

O'er lone savannahs I have pass'd,
And on their sea-like broad gray-green
   The mantle of my glory cast ;
Have strewn the splendour of my sheen
   On tops of forests whose deep heart
I pierce whene'er my shaft so keen
   Can find a vulnerable part.

8.

And sometimes, as the merry earth
Goes reeling round, I steal a glance
   At scenes of revelry and mirth ;
Peep into courtly halls perchance,
   Where, midst some glittering concourse, trace
The intricacies of the dance
   With rhythmic movement forms of grace.

9.

Rich marbles, paintings ; heaped with rare
Exotics every space recess'd,
   Which human flowers brush past, more fair—
Youth, maid, when clinging breast to breast
   In giddy whirl ; light laughter's chime,
And hum of tongues, by clash suppress'd
   Of instruments from time to time ;—

10.

Young faces flushed with pleasure's glow ;
The flash of gems on many a throat
  And bosom stainless as the snow ;
Stars, ribbons which the brave denote ;
  The shifting of a thousand hues ;
Gay robes, bright glances, locks afloat ;
  The light a thousand lamps diffuse :—

11.

Oh, radiant scene !—They shut me out
With jealous care, because they think
  At touch of my pure sheen, no doubt,
Their mimic day would wane and shrink.
  In vain ! a curtain pulled aslant,
Or some unnoticed shutter-chink,
  Affords me just the glimpse I want.

12.

I crossed but late a land which war
Was scourging, and beheld the spot
  Where two hosts met the day before ;
Dark heaps of dead the plain did dot,
  Horses and men ; I flung a pall
Snow-white, my frosty beam, o'er what
  Was their last bivouac of all.

13.

A ship on fire at dead of night
I saw in ocean's midst, a dread
    And woeful yet a splendid sight.
Miles round upon the sea was shed
    A bloody glare.   What men could do
To stanch the flames or stay their spread,
    That did, in vain, her gallant crew.

14.

I heard the shrieks, and saw the crush
And frantic struggle, as the poor
    Doomed, desperate creatures made a rush
To gain the boats ; in one no fewer
    Than thirty crowded, such a host
Swamping it straight, you may be sure ;
    The next turned bottom-uppermost.

15.

The mizen-mast, that giving way,
Though unperceived, some time had been,
    Fell on another just as they
Had launched her, braining those within.
    Two, made clear off ; what these befell,
And if 'twas e'er their fate to win
    Some shore in safety, who can tell ?

16.

Those who upon the burning deck
Remained might choose their mode of death,
  And as the flames, which nought could check,
Advancing scorched them with their breath,
  Or bursting forth in some fresh spot
Menaced their foot-hold underneath,
  They one by one the billows sought.

17.

With baby clasped to breast a mother
Over the burning bulwarks sprung ;
  Six children, one after the other,
Into the waves a father flung,
  Then plunged himself; the captain cast
His arms about the wife who hung
  Upon his neck and leapt in last.

18.

I saw afloat amid the seas
A raft two shipwrecked men which bore ;
  The brine immersed them to the knees ;
At times they'd doze, anon explore
  The distance ; either hugged the other
For warmth, and still the slow hours wore,
  And still each hour proved like its brother.

19.

Joy, joy ! a vessel looms in sight !
They hoist a coat upon an oar,
      And shout for help with all their might ;
It seemed as if the big ship bore
      Full down on them ; she grew so near,
Her paddles' stroke and engines' roar
      Amid the stillness they could hear.

20.

Poor signal, flaunting unobserved !
Poor voices, all in vain uplifted !
      And now it seemed her course had swerved,
Or was it they themselves had shifted ?
      Within a league of them at last—
Their fierce eyes saw from where they drifted
      Her glimmering cabin-lights—she pass'd !

21.

Within an attic, in a street
Obscure, a genius wrote for bread ;
      He dropped his pen and left his seat,
And tottering round his wretched bed
      Stood leaning on the window-sill,
. For me to kiss and bathe his head ;
      Haggard he looked, poor youth, and ill,

22.

With flushen cheek and flaming eye ;
In my cold way to comfort him
    I tried, but only made him sigh,
And caused his poor wild eyes to swim,
    By conjuring some home-scene to mind ;
So straightway left the garret dim,
    And hid again a cloud behind.

23.

Two gentle worshippers of mine
The sea marge sought, to watch me rise
    And on the tranquil waters shine ;
And both at meeting feigned surprise,
    Just as though each had been the one
Whom least of all the other's eyes
    Expected to have lighted on.

24.

The girl blushed rosy-red, no less
Confused the youth appeared than she did ;
    And both betrayed more nervousness
Than, as it seemed, the occasion needed ;
    They paced together to and fro
In converse soft, and never heeded
    Whether the moon was up or no !

O

25.

In many a fateful assignation
· I make a third.   Last night was one.
    Two voices in fierce altercation
Adown a lonely lane.   Anon
    A blade's outflash; a freezing cry;
A thud—a moan—a gurgle; on
    The furious deed none looked but I.

26.

I saw it as I peered athwart
The inky clouds that by me sped,
    Myself unseen.   The rack did part
At length and pass, storm-piloted.
    He knew himself the child of hell
He was—that murderer, on his dead
    When my accusing splendour fell.

27.

The shadow of the hedge-row, thrown
Sharply along the narrow road,
    The patches where the grass had grown,
The cart-wheel's furrow—all I showed;
    The hurrying clouds; the rill that sweet
And clear beside the pathway flowed;
    The bloody thing against his feet.

28.

Chill sweat-beads to his forehead came ;
He viewed his hands, all smeared with red ;
   He called his victim by her name ;
Then started off with dizzy head ;
   He gained the fields, a moment stood
Uncertain, then across them fled
   As if a pack of fiends pursued.

29.

If I could only tell one half
Of what I see in one short night,
   The world would wonder, weep, and laugh
As never yet, and well it might ;
   Did any subtle poet ken
All earth discloses to my sight,
   How he might thrill the hearts of men !

FUGITIVE VERSES.

SPRING.

AFTER a spell of cold gray cloudy weather,
　　What can be pleasanter than when at last
One day the Winter ceases altogether,
And Spring, with bursting buds, and genial skies,
Warm Spring, breaks on us like a sweet surprise ;—
To watch the lambs in meadows frisk, to hear
The song o'erhead of sky-lark, joyous-clear,
　　And note flit lightly past
The first pale yellow butterfly of the year.

Season of birth and resurrection !—waking
The earth out of her Winter trance, and making
Her dormant energies begin to stir ;
Teaching the sap to feel its silent way
　　Into the topmost twig,
The embryo plant to break its sepulchre,
And pierce the mould sweet air and light to gain.
　　Season of hope and happy promise !—big
With golden possibilities ; the gay
And lavish Flora dancing in thy train.

The crisped and sparkling surface of the deep
 With swift weird wing the new-come swallow skims;
Out of their winter hiding-places creep
The tortoise—dormouse—not a living thing
But feels thy quick'ning influence, O Spring!
There is melodious contest going on
In every wood, and, when some prize is won,
 Chanting of marriage hymns:
The songless birds their wedding plumage don.

The blazing noon-tide Summer is more splendid;
A deeper and diviner tone is blended
With Autumn's harmony; but thou art best—
When happy creatures link them to their kind,
 Youth, morning of the year!
Thou of all seasons art the welcomest—
Lovely and tender as the infant green
 Of thine own buds!—for Love doth use to appear,
His hand—thou leading him—with thine entwin'd;
And Death, a distant shade, is hardly seen.

APRIL.

'GREEN buds and snowy orchard blooms appear,—
  The Spring is near;
But my heart keeps its winter all the year.

The scent of hidden violets comes and goes;
  The sweet primrose
And daffodil that hangs its head, unclose;—

Now in dim woodland dells may these be found,
  Lighting the ground
With pallid beauty everywhere around.

The trees their vernal garb once more assume;
  The yellow broom
By lone waysides is breaking into bloom;

The lilac is in bud; larks soar and sing;
  Next month will bring
The swallow, without whom 'tis scarcely Spring.

Again to life and song the woods awake;
  The birds forsake
Their Winter haunts, and build in bush and brake.

Ah, happy birds! that know no wild regret—
  That love, and yet
That, having loved, are able to forget!

BY THE SEA.

Oɴ either hand
A sweep of tawny sand
With gentle curve extending, smooth and wide,
On which bold rocks look down
With dark and sullen frown,
Slopes out to meet the fast incoming tide.

The sunbeams leap
And frolic o'er the deep,
And, where their light is most intensely pour'd,
Strike from its surface keen
Flashes of diamond sheen,
Dazzling the eyes that gaze out thitherward.

A cloud or two
Drifts lightly 'mid the blue ;
And, like a faint white blot upon the sky,
Up yonder you can trace
The day moon's dim drowned face,
Whose light will flood all heaven by-and-by.

The rhythmical
Hoarse sounds that rise and fall,
Thund'rous, upon the ear from out at sea,
The tumult nearer land,
And splash upon the sand
Of breaking waves, compose one harmony.

AN INVITATION IN JULY.

COME out with me, come out with me,
And watch the sunset from the sea.
Where is the boat, you wish to know?
  The boat is sleeping on its side,
  On the tawny sand up which the tide
Is crawling in the cove below.

Come out with me, come out—the moon,
That all the sultry afternoon
  Looked like the ghost of herself as she lay
Whelmed in the blue, will be stealing soon
  Pale fire from the dying torch of day,
  And paving with her light the way
For those who wander o'er the deep ;
  And the silver stars by twos and threes
Out of the gathering shades will peep
To view themselves in the waters fair ;
  And what is more, a gentle breeze
  Begins to blow delightfully—
    You can see it yonder sweeping o'er
    The liquid golden floor

Of the dying sun's superb pavilion,
   Breaking its smoothness up into a million
  Small diamond sparkles—come with me,
Come out and taste the fresh'ning air.

One shall steer and one shall row,
('Then we'll be face to face, you know,)
And o'er the water we will go,
And have such talk the while!—I trow
About all things in earth and heaven :
   Sometimes we'll pause, and for a spell
Sit watching the mild face of even,
Gleaning such lore from her sweet looks
As is not to be found in books,
   Which some we know love all too well ;
Or listening to the curlew's cry,
   Piercing the stillness near at hand,
As silently we drift hard by
   The reedy margin of the land.

LEILA.

WHERE is Leila fled?
Ask the wind that overhead
　Stirred the branches of the thorn,
While was planned in whispers low
Her stealthy flight three nights ago :
　This should be Leila's marriage morn ;
But Leila fled away
Ere the first golden ray
Over the hill-tops ushered in the day.

Where is Leila fled?
Ask the eastern star that shed
　From out a heaven all flushed with rose,
Dappled with clouds of pearl, its light
Silvern and mild, on Leila's flight ;
　Ask that bright witness if it knows
Her haven of retreat,
Who should step forth to meet
A bridegroom on this young May morning sweet.

Why had Leila flown ?
And flew the fugitive alone ?
　The bridegroom he was gray and old,

Leila was young, and I suspect
She fled away with her heart's elect ;
   Leila cared more for love than gold,
Hence, without word of warning,
To sell her high heart scorning,
She fled away upon her bridal morning.

FOUR SONGS.

—:o:—

AUBADE.

THAT silver star, so fair, that shone
Among the opal clouds of dawn,
    It disappeared three hours agone ;
The dew is glistening on the lawn ;
      And one you love is loitering here
      Beneath your window, dear.

The flowers uphold their heads, each one
Heavy with night's crystalline wine,
    For morning kisses of the sun,
As you will hold up yours for mine
      When you descend, and find me here
      Beneath your window, dear.

Each time it blows this way the gale
Outshakes the jasmine's breath so sweet,
    And strews its blossoms fair and frail
Upon the ground against my feet,
      My idle feet, that loiter here,
      Beneath your window, dear.

I hear the lark's impulsive lay
From sunny regions overhead,
 The rivulet at baby-play
Among the pebbles in its bed ;
 The bees hum past me—loitering here
 Beneath your window, dear.

Come forth ! the morn is young like you,
And youth, ah youth so swiftly flies !—
 The breeze is fresh, the sky is blue,
Only less blue than are the eyes
 For whose sweet sake I loiter here,
 Beneath your window, dear.

CLOUD.

A CLOUD the sky has overspread,
The brightness of the landscape fled,
  A chill is in the air;
The sea has turned a wannish gray,
That flashing in the distance lay,
  One sapphire everywhere.

Oh, love! our heaven is darkened o'er;
We wander hand in hand no more
  While each to each imparts
The rising thought: we interchange
Words cold and few; our looks are strange
  And troubled like our hearts.

But though our sky be overcast,
I know this weather cannot last;
  I know the unruffled blue
Exists behind it all the while,
I know that, with relenting smile,
  The sun will struggle through.

WEEPING IN THE RAIN.

You stand there weeping in the rain !
Upbraid me, taunt me, if you choose,
Your cheek avert, your hand refuse,
   But, I implore, your tears restrain ;
Indulge your anger, exercise
Your scornful wit, but dry your eyes !

You stand there weeping in the rain !
Although your tears, you know full well,
Distress me more than words can tell ;
   To see them rives my heart in twain !
You love me not, or you would ne'er
Resort to weapons so unfair.

I own 't was I that was to blame ;
The jealous thought that barbed my tongue
To wound you, and from yours which wrung
   Such sharp retort, I here disclaim ;
For Love's sweet sake forgive me, see !--
I ask it upon bended knee.

The hedge-row glistens with the sheen
Of myriad rain-drops—lo, once more
The sun shines, though the shower's scarce o'er :
    The meadow wears its liveliest green ;
Must the returning sunshine view
Dissension between me and you ?

    The birds all round are singing loud
For joy that heaven again has smiled ;
All things save we are reconciled ;
    Observe the bow in yon dark cloud,—
Methinks that bow is meant to be
A sign of peace 'twixt you and me.

    'T were sure, this music of our life,
Without some discords incomplete ;
But be that as it may, so sweet
    Is reconcilement after strife,
You will remember without pain
How you stood weeping in the rain.

SERENADE.

THE day looks flushed and weeps a little shower
  At parting, as if parting made it grieve ;
Love, you and I within this transient hour
  Of one the other must be taking leave,—
Your cheek yon cloud's contagious rose has caught,
Your gentle eyes brim over at the thought.
    Day of my life ! no sorrow,—
    We meet again to-morrow.

There is an end to every lovely thing,
  And so this sweetest day is gone for ever ;
Life is all cadenced, throbbing to the swing
  Of some mysterious rhythm—hands clasp, to sever
Lips cling, to part ; the tide that buoys the bark
Ebbs and then flows ; the dawn succeeds the dark :
    We yet shall live beholden
    For other days as golden.

A LULLABY.

Lullaby !
What the wind says to the flower
   As it rocks it on its stem :
" Loth day weeps a farewell shower ;
   Haggard clouds the sunset hem,
  Afterflushed with angry rose ;
  Furl your petals, furl them close.
      Lullaby !
      Eve is nigh ! "

Lullaby !
What the bird sings to its nestlings,
   Cradled in the fir-tree's fork :
" Half-fledged pinions, cease your wrestlings,
   Soon the winds will give you work ;
  Struggling throats be mute, ere long
  You shall wake the woods with song.
      Lullaby !
      Dusk is nigh ! "

Lullaby !
Sings the mother to the baby
  Pillowed softly on her breast :
" Slumber, dear ; till risen the day be
  Nought disturb your tranquil rest ;
Veil those stars of morn, your eyes,
Till morn's star is in the skies.
    Lullaby !
    Night is nigh ! "

Lullaby !
What my heart, dejected, hears
  Love in gentlest accents utter :
" Sleep, babe, tired 'twixt play and tears ;
  Wild bird, cease your wings to flutter ;
Flower that looked upon the sun,
Fold your leaves, the day is done.
    Lullaby ;
    Death is nigh !"

GARTH'S SONG.

When dawn's opal tints have fled,
With the glamour that they shed,
And, as we fare on together,
Clouds obscure the golden weather;
When the wind blows cold and rude,
And the storm must be withstood,—
Darling, if our lips then meet,
Will my kisses seem as sweet?

When the brow is creased with care;
When the frost invades the hair;
When the cheek's rose-bloom is vanished,
And the lovelight has been banished
From the eyes by time and tears;
In those late, unlovely years,
Darling, if our lips should meet,
Will my kisses seem as sweet?

When high hope, which lured from far,
Proves a meteor, not a star;
When ambitions have miscarried;
When the flesh to pain is married,
And a sword has pierced the soul;
When we near life's dim, dread goal,—
Darling, if our lips then meet,
Will my kisses seem as sweet?

BONNIE MAY.

Bonnie May, bonnie May,
Why are you in tears to-day,
Who are wont to be so gay?

There are tears than smiles more sweet;
There are sorrows which to meet
Maidens go with willing feet.

There are wounds which will not heal
Till a second time they feel
Touch them the remorseful steel.

Lips that wounded you before,
Will you let them now restore—
Touch you into health once more?

Lips know best wherewith to atone
For offences of their own—
Lips themselves when contrite grown.

Mine that chid now fain would kiss;
Lo, the sorrow I dismiss
From your eyes with this—and this.

After shower the sunshine's ray;
Tears to joyous smiles give way;
Bonnie May, bonnie May!

SONG FOR SIR TRISTRAM.

FELLOW EXILE, you with me are interdicted Love's
dominions ;

Is there nowhere priest or potentate can take away the
ban ?

Ah, re-enter might we, shielded by some pitying angel's
pinions

Just for one brief day—hour—moment !—from the frown
of God and man !

Must I never in your eyes behold the lovelight sparkle,
never ?

Must I never seek your lips with mine again throughout
all time ?

Within all the earth's green confines is there no place,
none whatever,

Where as lovers you and I may meet and greet without a
crime ?

There is one place,—but I fear, sweet, the blue daylight
will be wanting,

And the brook's song, and the garden's honeyed scents
and glowing dyes ;

No bird's warble, no young sunbeam through a latticed
window slanting,

Will awake us from our slumber when the morn is in the
skies.

There is one great angel—he puts wide divorce 'twixt
other lovers,

But he brings us two together—he alone, and lets us
blend,

While his broad wings' brooding darkness overshadows
us and covers,

In one silent, unforbidden, close embrace that knows no
end.

LOVE AND HOPE.

I saw Love seated on a rock, with Hope
   Dead at his feet. A uniform gray screen
Of cloud concealed the young day's azure cope ;

   No wind-sown flower, no leaf, no blade of green
Grew near ; the naked rocks, the leaden sky,
   And those two shapes alone composed the scene.

Tears on his cheek, but none within his eye,—
   Whose lightnings now all spent or smothered were,—
For he had wept until their source was dry,

   With drooping pinion, drooping head, an air
Of utter desolation in his mien,
   Grief for the moment yielding to despair,

And hands loose-clasped that hung his knees between—
   He sat, his form appearing to exhale
A wan and wavering splendour, which was seen

   To clothe his round smooth limbs with lustre pale,
And flicker mid his bright and clustering hair,
   Quick'ning its gold to flame, but which did fail

To pierce the shadow that enshrouded there
   Where outstretched at his feet it lay, ay me !—
That other figure, feminine and fair,

   Whose cruel death caused all his misery.
   Alas for Love, when Hope has ceased to be !

A BOY'S PORTRAIT.

A BOY of twelve years old or thereabout,
Tall for his age, with womanly-white hands,
And one of those rare faces which recall
Some Phidian fragment in their modelling,
So cleanly chiselled that they never change
Materially, and are beautiful
From birth till death.   Brown hair just tinged with gold,
Clust'ring in natural curls round temples pale ;
Broad level brows with shadows under them ;
A look of sweet and innocent gravity
In his gray eyes—a listening eagerness
About his lips.

           A quiet, thoughtful lad,
Less pleased to mingle in the playground sports
Than sit apart and pore on some old book,
And weave the dreams that wrapped him from the
    world ;
Who, notwithstanding such unsocial ways,
Was half a favourite with his wild compeers,
For he was gentle, frank, and knew not fear.
A sweet recluse amid the schoolboy throng ;
A hermit-child whose cave was his own mind.

WHO?

Who likes his name, his features, or his lot?
 Who values his own gifts, howe'er endow'd,
And oft with vain repining envies not
 Now this now that one singled from the crowd?

Who that has thirsted for renown achieves it
 While most worth having—early in life's day?
The laurel having nobly earned, receives it
 On locks whose gold is yet unflecked with gray?

Who, patient seeker after fame eternal,
 Wielding the brush, the chisel, or the pen,
Walks while his years (ah, happy!) still are vernal,
 Crowned with high recognition among men?

Who weds, and though he wed through fortune's kind-
  ness
 The one beloved, ne'er feels his chain a weight,
And never sheds the scales of happy blindness?
 Who meets and marries with his soul's true mate?

Who—why continue? Such how rare! men wed
 The earthly Venus; fame its tardy praise
Blares o'er the hero's bloody grave; the head
 Is bald or silvered when it wears the bays.

STANZAS.

What do I care for lark or nightingale,—
　Babble of unseen waters, hum of bees
That stagger in and out the lilies pale
　On drowsy afternoons, or symphonies
Heroical, or airs the most divine
　Of Gluck or Mozart, what care I for these,
When I can hear discourse that voice of thine?

What do I reck of moon or star? The skies
　Of midnight, when high winds have swept them bare,
Mirrored within some tarn that sheltered lies
　Among its mountains, dark and still, are fair;
And fine it is to watch the moon arise,
　And sweet—but all things lovely whatsoe'er
Fade into nought when I behold thine eyes.

What is the beauty of the world to me—
　Splendour of sunsets; opalescent tints
Of gracious dawns; in storm or calm the sea;
　The hectic hues of Autumn; softest glints
And pencils, shed through boughs that interlace,
　Of gold-green light; the earliest day that hints
Of Spring—if thou but turn to me thy face?

MY TOWN.

My town, beside its own fair waters seated,
  Whose wharves and sun-tipped spires and shining bay
The wanderer, sick for sight of home, has greeted
  With joyful tears of welcome many a day.

The port of sad farewells and happy meetings ;
  Each street, and church, and shop, how well I know—
Its docks where, punctual as the pulse's beatings,
  The monster ocean mail-ships come and go.

Its breeze-swept common—where is gorse so golden,
  Or May so fragrant?—with whose sod, our pain
All o'er, we blend at last ; its gateways olden,
  And hoary walls that recollect the Dane.

My birthplace, like a living thing extended
  Along the margin of its waters, where
The glow of Autumn sunsets is so splendid,
  The sheen of Summer moonlight is so fair!

Each week the tranquil street, so long the centre
  On which my world revolved, once more I pace,
And pass the house I dare no longer enter—
  Ghosts haunt it which I cannot bear to face.

Yet fancy oft reverts and round it hovers ;
  I dwell there still and all things seem the same ;
I hear the tread of feet the clay now covers,
  And voices, hushed for ever, call my name.

I pitch a tent elsewhere since Time, the Vandal,
  Destroyed my household hearth ; yet still I own,
With all its social gossip, sin, and scandal,
  I love it—home the first, and last—*my* town.

August, 1884.

IN MEMORY OF G. S.

Died at Portsea, December 19th, 1881.   Aged 16 years.

BRING blossoms fresh and virginal and sweet,
And buds half-blown—such best the occasion meet,
    And strew them
Lightly upon this new-made grave, and let
Tears of the warmest, tenderest regret
    Bedew them ;
And holly too, the season to betoken :
  For she was fresh and sweet and virginal,
  And she was plucked in her young bloom withal,
Who sleeps beneath these sods so lately broken.

The poor young voice is mute, but yet its clear
Last notes seem still to vibrate on my ear
    And linger ;
No praise of mine or others where she dwells
Can overtake her now, and no farewells,
    My singer !
Flowers were her latest gifts to me, unfaded
  When she too drooped ; so scant the leave she stay'd
  To take, so brief the parting that she made—
Flower-like herself—she died as soon as they did.

Had any one forewarned us there was hid
That cypress-bud this Christmas-tide amid
     Our holly,—
Had any short while since predicted thus,
We must have smiled and cried, incredulous,
     " What folly ! "
Dead with the dying year ; the shades that thicken
  Are stabbed with shafts of dawn around its close,
  And not of death but birth are half its throes ;
But her—ah, her no April skies re-quicken !

FAST FRIENDS.

(Soudan. January, 1885.)

THE same towers sheltered them in infancy;
They learnt to say their prayers at the same knee.

From sources close akin their blood they drew;
Had toys, games, books in common as they grew.

In boyish sports with equal ardour blended;
Later in loving rivalry contended

For honours of the schools. But, youth just past,
A feeling shared in common came at last

Their friendship's current smooth to cross and stem;—
Both loved one woman, and that sundered them.

They joined opposing factions in the state;
And party rancour sharpened private hate.

Years sped; and then their enmity made pause
Beneath the standard of a gallant cause.

They melted—each to each did kind amends,
Hand wringing hand—and grew once more fast friends.

Fast friends.   One ship conveyed them to the shore
Of that dread continent they left no more.

They marched in the same column, through the wide
Parched land forlorn, to battle side by side.

They met the furious onslaught of the foe
Shoulder to shoulder, their two breasts aglow

With one high hope; and where they fell, athirst
The desert sand of that black clime accurst

Drank their commingling blood.   Among the slain,
Shoulder to shoulder, on the battle-plain

That night they lay,—wide eyes, with cold blind stare,
Turned to the alien stars.
                    Fast friends elsewhere?

LINES

For the first anniversary of General Gordon's death.
January 26th, 1886.

ONE year this dawn, at dawn's red signal ray,
  The dusk fanatics of the desert poured
  Into the fallen city—that fierce horde
Held all those painful strenuous months at bay ;
  And failure and defeat, unique in story,
  Crowned one dead brow with such undying glory
As laurelled Cæsars miss.   A year to-day.

The wearer of the charmèd life struck down
  By bloody death !   What tempest, past belief,
  Then swept the land, of rage, remorse, and grief !
And still, west, east, where'er its fame has flown,
  From far Cathay unto the Golden Gate,
  At that proud sacrifice men's hearts vibrate,
Glow at its splendour o'er its shame to groan.

On this your birthday morn among the dead—
  Greeting.   (The dead ? the dead are we, not they.)
  Your birthday in some realm of ampler day,

Where haply new and clearer paths you tread
   Of high heroical experience;
   From us, who yearned to save, to you, snatched hence
In scorn by force less laggard and more dread.—

To you beyond the gulf, behind the veil—
   So black, impervious, yet perchance so thin.
   Your place lies void among your buried kin.
Your nation cannot claim your dust. The tale
   Is all perplexed of how you passed from men.
   But splendid, flawless is your fame. Again—
Greeting, great Pacha! birthday greeting. Hail!

To W. C. and L. C. C.

To you, in memory of the vanished days,
   This volume I devote, to both and each;
   You whom no echo of my songs may reach;
You too remote to blame them or to praise.

For all the tender toil wherewith you strove
   To pave for me the world's uneven way:
   The halcyon years my dreaming shallop lay
Moored in the shining haven of your love.

The joy with which you watched my mind unfold,
   And shaped its inchoate thought; the gracious lore
   Whose fountains you unsealed; for all you bore
And forbore, all the vigilant cares untold

And pains profuse you lavished, matchless friends!—
   In nurturing that one fledgeling of the nest;
   This book is yours, imperfect thanks at best,
And with the letters of your names it ends.

Henderson, Rait, & Spalding, Printers, 3 & 5, Marylebone Lane, London, W.